# The EARL ON THE TRAIN

# KERRIGAN BYRNE

The Earl On the Train Copyright © 2022 Kerrigan Byrne

Published by Oliver-Heber Books

0 9 8 7 6 5 4 3 2 1

*One*

**SEBASTIAN MONCRIEFF PALMED** his blade in the darkness, anticipating a kill.

He waited, listening to the boisterous night, savoring the sensation of the ground moving beneath him.

Always moving.

In fact, the only time he felt unstable was when he stood in one place.

He'd built sea legs as the first mate on one of the most famous—er *infamous*—ships in the entire world, The Devil's Dirge. Now that the Rook had regrettably retired, Moncrieff sought other ways to keep ahead of the relentless demons giving him chase.

To keep the ground beneath him from falling away.

The fastest steamships, most expensive coaches, wildest stallions, and even a novelty such as a hot air balloon provided escape from the prison to which he'd been sentenced.

For the next three days, it was the clack and sway of a train mobilizing the floor beneath his feet. The sumptuous luxury locomotive followed the tracks of the Orient Express from London to Constantinople.

He'd booked his passage with the intent to assassinate one Arthur Weller.

As luck would have it, he'd the opportunity to do it tonight, before the train even reached Paris, with no one the wiser. For the rest of the trip to Constantinople, he'd sit back and watch the resulting chaos whilst indulging in expensive cigars and baccarat, before retiring to his private car.

Where he'd sleep with the unburdened conscience of an innocent baby.

At least where Arthur Weller was concerned.

He'd plenty of sin staining his soul, and plenty of ghosts to haunt his dreams...but they'd be silent tonight.

They always were after these kills.

Arthur Weller eschewed a rail steward, preferring to be attended by his personal valet. Thus, no one stood sentinel as Sebastian let himself into the railcar, shaking the skiff of snow from his hair.

His own accommodations were three cars away, as only an idiot would murder his neighbor and not expect suspicion.

No one, however, would imagine someone would be mad enough to let himself out onto the landing of the speeding train, and proceed to climb onto the roof in order to leap several cars forward.

Few people built their strength spidering about a ship for a decade, clinging to dubious handholds while the sea did its level best to claim anyone foolish enough to be out in a gale.

Compared to a steamship in a hurricane, the roof of a train might as well have been a stroll in Hyde Park.

It had rails and everything.

Measuring his breath, Sebastian flattened his back against the wall of the Weller's first-class car and peeked around the corner to assure no one moved about the narrow hall. Unlikely at this hour, but one never knew if a family member needed a midnight snack or use of the necessary.

One wouldn't want a murder interrupted by something so pedestrian as a wee.

Empty. *Excellent.*

The lone lamp provided little better than a golden well for shadows, and Sebastian melded with them as he crept along the hallway.

Three doors shielded the opulent cabin suites in which the Weller family slept. According to the information he'd paid handsomely for, Arthur Weller's cabin was the last one on the right.

The knife felt like his own appendage as he passed the first door belonging to Weller's daughter, and the middle cabin in which his wife, Adrienne, slept.

He pressed his ear to Weller's door and listened for any movement before sliding it open and easing inside. The elite nobles could hardly abide squeaks, and God love the well-oiled luxury of first-class. It made stealing about so much easier.

The drapes had been left open, revealing the meager glow of the city as it reflected off the delicate flakes of snow to mingle with various lights from the train. It illuminated just enough of the cabin to outline the shadows of furniture and glint off crystal, silver, and his blade.

Tucking the knife against his cuff, Sebastian slithered closer to his mark.

The vile fuck would finally get what was coming to him. Perhaps he should light a lamp so he could watch the life bleed from Weller's eyes.

Sebastian had never been a macabre sort of fellow.

He left that to men with darker predilections. But this...*this* was personal.

Drifting to the bed, he loomed over the outline of a slim body, his every muscle coiled like a snake.

When he struck, it was with a viper's speed and precision, and before his victim could blink from slumber to awareness, he'd a knife to his throat and arms pinned helplessly to his side.

*Wait.*

He released one alarmingly slim arm to test a curious softness he'd not expected.

*Breasts. Shit.*

"Please." The feminine plea feathered over his flesh and arrowed down his breastbone, landing in his cock. "Please, no."

Lord, but he loved it when they begged.

Begged for pleasure, to be precise, never for their lives.

*This* was a disconcerting development, to say the least.

Sebastian snatched his offending hand away from the lovely orb with no small amount of reluctance and regret. The shape had fit his palm like a dream, the warmth of the plentiful flesh beneath a thin cotton night rail a balm to his frozen fingers. The plump nipple beaded against the cold.

Who was this, the wife or the daughter? Thinking swiftly, he returned the knife to his cuff with the swiftest sleight of hand. If he was lucky, he could rely on what he always did to get out of trouble with a lady.

His charm and general magnificence.

"Do pardon me, madam, or is it miss? I fear I have the wrong railcar." He released her carefully and straightened, hoping to convey chagrin from the shadows. "I was...invited by a woman, you see, and this is the car number she gave me along with orders to be stealthy. I dare think we both might have been had."

"Moncrieff?"

The disbelieving whisper froze the blood in his veins and his tongue to the roof of his mouth.

*That voice.*

He'd recognize it anywhere. Heard it in his most salacious dreams.

And the mild ones, as well.

Her features were little better than shadows, but it didn't matter. He'd committed her every feature to memory more than a year ago. The curve of her cheekbone, sharp yet delicate. The silk of her ebony hair and the cream of her skin.

The veritable perfection of her incomparable beauty.

Veronica Weatherstoke.

A woman possessed of every virtue he'd lost along the way.

She was loyal, erudite, patient, measured, clever, strong...

*Kind.*

It was rare for such a beautiful woman to develop such deep wells of compassion, rarer still a countess. Hers was not a refined sort of empathy.

She'd been born into this merciless world with a tender heart, soft eyes the color of the finest jade, and a full, kind mouth...

The *kind* of mouth he often pictured stretched around his cock.

His astonishment gave her time to sit upright, clutching the covers over her pale, high-necked gown.

"Sebastian Moncrieff, what the devil are you doing here?" she hissed in a loud whisper.

5

"I told you, seducing the wrong woman, apparently." Or the right one, if fortune favored his cursed soul.

"With that knife you hid up your cuff?"

"Saw that, did you?" Fortune, he remembered, was a fickle bitch.

"One does not forget the feel of steel against one's throat."

Sebastian had never before put a blade to her lily-white throat.

Which meant someone else had.

Just as he was about to inquire as to the name of the dead man walking, she said, "Tell me the truth, Moncrieff. What are you doing here?"

"Attempting to kill Arthur Weller," he answered blithely. "What are *you* doing his cabin? Wait..." He swallowed a surge of bile as he calculated the possibilities with abject disgust. "Tell me you're not warming his bed. I'll slit my wrists right now if you and he—"

"I'd rather warm my innards with a hot poker than the likes of *Arthur Weller*." She said the name as if it tasted rotten in her mouth.

*Thank Christ.* He'd known she had more scruples than to take such a cretin as a lover. Did she have a lover? He wondered. Was she in need of one?

He certainly would apply for the position.

For *every* position she would allow.

"W-what will you do now?" she asked, a tremulous hint of vulnerability escaping on her voice. He could see her clearer now, the outline of her dark braid, the motions of her lips. Just shapes and shades, and no less alluring for it.

"I've hardly made up my mind," he confessed, wondering what she'd do if he kissed her.

Would she submit to his seduction, yielding that soft body to his skillful caresses?

Or would she knee him in the nads?

With a jerking, almost violent motion, she tossed the bedclothes off and scrambled to her feet, standing before him with her shoulders thrown back in challenge. "I *refuse* to become a prisoner of yours again, do you hear me, you villainous troll?"

"*Technically*, you were a prisoner of my captain, the Rook," he corrected indulgently, placing a hand over his heart to advertise where she'd wounded him.

If he were possessed of a heart.

"And...*troll*?" he tutted. "I *hardly* believe that's an apropos comparison. Trolls are unsightly and unwashed, famously living beneath bridges and such nonsense. Whereas I am fastidiously clean and have been told I'm at least tolerably attractive." Words like masculine perfection, Adonis, Eros, and even the title *handsomest man alive* had been bandied about, but manners dictated he remain humble. "Let us find another villainous creature to assign to me."

"Ogre, then," was her next suggestion.

"My Lady, I don't mean to hound a point, but surely you're aware ogres and trolls are in good company together. Might I suggest—"

She splayed her hands against his chest and pushed with all her adorable strength. He even let her budge him a little, to soothe her ire.

"Whatever fiendish demon you find acceptable, I care not! Either kill me or... Get. *Out*."

Sebastian hissed in a breath through his teeth. "I'm in a bit of a conundrum, you see, as I can't seem to do either. We *both* know I won't kill you...

"Oh, do we?"

When he realized she might not be able to read his sardonic look in the dimness, he made an audible sound conveying his impatience. "Secondary, I cannot allow you to alert Weller to my plans...so what to do with you, is the question." He tapped a thoughtful finger on his chin.

"You do nothing *with* or *to* me, you piratical bastard. Touch me again and I'm going to scream until my breath runs out."

*Bastard?* She had no idea.

"Go ahead." He shrugged. "The first person who comes through that door catches my blade. So, I very much hope it's no one you're overly fond of."

"You pigeon-livered ratbag!"

Reaching out, he caught her hand before it connected with his cheek. "Come now, don't let's dwell on the past. Tell me where Weller is, I'll slit his throat and be out of your hair before dawn."

She snatched her fingers away cringing toward the bed. "My *God*, but you're cold."

"Trust me, woman, if you knew Arthur Weller's sins, you'd be sending him to Hell yourself."

"No, I mean, you're as frozen as a corpse."

"Apologies. It is beginning to snow out there, and I had to use my hands to steady myself so as not to fall off the roof."

A beat of silence passed. Then another. "The roof?" she echoed, as if she'd never before heard the word.

"How else would I attain entry to the car undetected?"

"I—I couldn't say." Lifting her hands, she scrubbed them over her face a few times, as if to wipe away stress, or sleep, or the sight of Sebastian, himself. "Why do you want to kill Arthur Weller?"

"For all the reasons you don't seem surprised, I expect," he replied darkly, as he realized that a provocative question had yet to be answered. "You never told me what you're doing in his bed."

She snorted with derision. "This isn't his bed, it's his daughter Penelope's."

Sebastian swallowed once. Twice. Momentarily paralyzed by lascivious images of what she and Arthur Weller's young daughter got up to in bed. "I never took you for a Jack the Lass... Lucky Penelope."

She instantly crossed her arms. "No, you rank *pervert*, I'm both her chaperone on this journey to meet her betrothed in Bucharest, *and* I'm designing the wedding trousseau."

"Hmmm..." he drew out the speculative sound. "Do you suppose there will still be a wedding once her father is dead? What is the requisite mourning period in Romania?"

She stared at him with her arms crossed over her breasts for an uncomfortably long time. The silence ate at him, as it was wont to do. The stillness swirling with the ghosts of his sins ready to catch him up.

He needed to move. To do something.

And here they were in the dark, with a bed. Him, shivering with the cold, and her, all warm and soft and effectively naked. What rotten fucking luck. The one woman who would likely never permit him to touch her.

The one woman he did his best to forget...if only his dreams would allow it.

"Moncrieff..." She hesitated, and his breath refused to draw at the sound of his name on her lips, spoken with a return of her innate gentility.

*My name is Sebastian.* He wanted her to say it. Over. And over. And again. He wanted her to sigh it. To moan it.

To scream it.

She ventured a step closer, beguiling him with the whisper of cotton against the bare skin beneath. "I'd say after everything you put me and Lorelai through, you might agree that you owe me a boon—"

"Come now," he interrupted. "I was properly careful that not one hair on your head was harmed on that ship—"

"Could you kill him tomorrow night, instead?"

*Two*

IT TOOK a great deal to stun Sebastian. Most often something cataclysmic. But hearing such a request from her lips did the trick. "Let me make certain I'm comprehending you, my lady." He held up a hand. "You're not asking me to spare Arthur Weller's life. Only to wait to murder him until tomorrow night."

"You heard correctly."

He cocked his head, thoroughly bemused. "I've never been more curious in my life as to someone's motives. You are not a murderer. In fact, I remember you begging the Rook to spare my life after I organized a mutiny against him, and abducted his wife, your sister-in-law, as collateral."

"I fully remember what you did," she said crisply. "But as you mentioned, Arthur Weller is a man who deserves the worst a villain like you could do to him. In fact, I have already hatched a plan to spirit his wife and daughter away. All I ask is time to do so before you send him to Hell."

*A villain like you.*

Sebastian had always been more than happy to play the scoundrel. He'd never let his roguish reputation

11

bother him in the least—in fact, he'd nurtured the status with vigor, until he was considered the perfect mélange of Guy Fawkes, Sir Francis Drake, and Cassanova.

Most women found him irresistible.

But not Veronica Weatherstoke.

Sebastian remembered watching as the Rook slid a dagger into her husband's brain. Her reaction to the murder had been horrified.

And yet, she'd not shed a single tear for the man.

The Earl of Southbourne, Mortimer Weatherstoke, had shanghaied an injured boy and sold him to a captain in need of a crew. The boy who'd become the Rook, the most terrible pirate in this century. Mortimer had broken his own sister Lorelai's leg over a toy, and killed her beloved pet rabbits before feeding them to her in a stew. He'd separated the Rook and Lorelai for twenty years on a cruel whim.

What must he have been like as a husband to Veronica?

As it always did, the thought hit him like a hammer to the guts, and the urge to commit murder surged to a fever pitch. "Where is Weller now?" he growled.

She flinched, and he instantly tempered his rage. "He's with his mistress somewhere in second class."

"Excellent. Why don't I simply find him and kill him tonight, and then his wife and daughter no longer have to worry? We can all sip Tuica in Bucharest by week's end."

Veronica shook her head vehemently before he'd finished his sentence. "Penelope doesn't *want* to marry the Romanian count to whom she is promised. The ink is dry on the contract. The dowry already sent. But if we can lose her in Paris, she can be married quickly to the man she truly loves, and on a ship bound for America by the time she is missed. Penelope is with him now, going over the plans for tomorrow night one last time."

"You trust this boy?" Sebastian asked.

She nodded. "He will care for her. He's young, but from a good family with plenty of means and, furthermore, decency. I know them from...from before."

"From when you were a countess?"

"From when I was nothing more than a shipping magnate's daughter with an obscene dowry of my own."

He made a soft sound in his throat. "I forgot you were not born nobility."

"I was *never* allowed to forget." The bleak note that stole into her voice tugged at the empty hole in his chest.

"Do you know the Wellers from then also?" he queried, Weller being a shipping magnate of his own.

"I had heard of him. He and my father were friendly rivals."

Sebastian's lip curled with distaste. "Did your father *also* take refugee and immigrant children and sell them to deviant men on far continents? Did he use his ships to smuggle stolen sarcophagi, relics, and pillaged art?"

"Of course not," she answered, horrified. "My father was an honorable man, but Weller is a brute and a bully. What he does to his own family is shameful enough, but to learn that he...that he is cruel to children..." She passed a hand over her eyes and then turned to him. "Are you, a *pirate*, really passing judgment? Do you see yourself as better than scum like Weller?"

"We were not those kinds of pirates," he defended. "We *took* from men like Weller. We had no quarrel with refugees or the poor, and often we freed them from such ships, and even added several to our crew."

"Oh *please*, don't make yourselves out to be some sort of Robin Hood figures. There is no such thing as a *good* pirate, and your lot were among the worst of them.

The Rook, at least, was redeemable because he'd been forced into the life, and everything he'd done was for Lorelai's sake."

Bending closer, he inhaled the scent of orchids and amber radiating from the warmth of her skin. God, but he hungered for a taste of her. Of every part of her that opened and bloomed. "I never claimed to be good, my lady—if anything, I am one of the most wicked men you'll ever know."

She retreated one step, which was all the space the tight quarters would allow. "I know you are wicked, which is why I don't trust you."

"I didn't ask you to."

"What do you mean?"

"Trust is a dangerous fallacy. The only thing I trust is that a person will always act in their own self-interest. Because of that, my lady, you can rely on me to keep my word in this respect. What is that old adage? The enemy of my enemy is my—"

"We are *not* friends."

"Uncomfortable allies, then," he offered. "You do what you have to do, Countess, and then I will rid the world of Arthur Weller."

"I'm not a countess any longer. I'm a dowager...little better than a seamstress now."

"Modesty doesn't suit you," he quipped. "You're becoming quite a name in the world of fashion."

"How do you know that?" The rank skepticism in her voice brought out a teasing smile he wished he could turn on her.

"Well, you kidnap a person once or twice and you tend to get attached," he admitted. "Tell me you haven't experienced something of the same issue. That you have not looked for mention of me here or there?"

She groaned with more disgust than the moment

warranted, in his opinion. "I'd all but forgotten you existed."

*Lies.*

Sebastian had many skills, and the chief among them was being able to tell when someone fed him a falsehood.

"Will I ever be anything but the villain to you, Veronica?" The question had left his lips before he could call it back.

"How could you not be?" She gestured wildly. "You turned on your captain and took my sister-in-law and best friend hostage during a mutiny. You threatened to kill her!"

He rolled his eyes. "I wouldn't have *done* it. Everyone knows that. I only needed to make a point."

"No one knows anything of the sort! How the devil did you escape prison? I was *certain* you'd have hanged for your crimes by now."

His brows met in confusion. "Surely you've heard."

"Heard what?"

She really didn't know? Oh, this was a *lark*.

"How long have you been on the Continent?" he asked.

"Since Ash married Lorelai, and don't you *dare* change the subject."

Ash. The Rook. His captain. His brother. His best friend. He'd have died for that man. He'd killed for that man. He'd hung his future, such as it was, upon the life they'd built at sea.

Only to have it disintegrated by the Rook's forgotten past. Ash had bound himself to a lost love and a brother he'd been twenty years without.

And Sebastian, his first mate and his most loyal friend, was set adrift.

And he might have acted...hastily. Now that time had separated him from the debacle, he had regrets.

Especially when it came to Veronica.

"I agree that I owe you this boon," he granted. "I will wait to assassinate Arthur Weller until you have carried out your plans."

"Thank you."

"Let us shake on it." He offered his hand.

"I'd rather not touch you."

Another lie.

*Interesting*...

"I'm glad we met again, Veronica. I didn't like how we parted." He couldn't remember the last time he'd said something so genuine. It made him feel exposed. Vulnerable.

He'd certainly not make a habit of it.

"You mean you disliked being led away in irons by Chief Inspector Morley?" she clarified with a syrupy sarcasm.

"I meant I regret you saw me like that. On the day I lost everything."

"On the day you *surrendered* everything," she corrected. "You brought it all on yourself, you know."

He knew.

It was a truth he often ran from, which meant he needed to get moving.

Yet, his feet didn't seem inclined to obey. He wasn't a man to look over his shoulder at the past, and yet... here she was. One of his most intrusive, pervasive memories.

So close.

So dangerously, alluringly close.

His heart sped. His breaths intensified as a dagger of dread threatened to skewer his tightening throat. If he thought about what he wanted to do, he'd take the deserter's road. He'd been many things in life, but a coward wasn't one of them.

Then why fear this? Fear her? What power did she have over him?

None.

Power was given or taken.

She wasn't the sort to take it. And he'd die before he gave it up. So, he needed to do this. It was what they both deserved.

"I'm sorry." The words tasted foreign and foul on his tongue, but he managed to spit them out.

It wasn't that he expected a parade or procession. Hell, he hadn't really even imagined forgiveness was forthcoming, but he thought she might have said *something* in return.

He groped about to fill the resulting silence. "I'm sorry," he repeated. "The thought that I might have frightened or distressed you offends me in every way."

"Thank you." Her reply was colored with astonishment.

With a practiced bow, Sebastian turned and eased the door back open, trying to ignore the warmth of her gaze on his chilly skin.

"Moncrieff," she called after him in an elevated whisper.

He paused, unable to turn around, half afraid she'd found the words to rebuke his apology.

"Do be careful on the roof. The snow is getting worse."

Sebastian didn't bother to fight the grin spreading across his face as he once again melded with the shadows.

Veronica Weatherstoke didn't want him to fall to his death from a speeding train.

And *that* felt like progress.

# Three

**VERONICA THOUGHT** she'd reached the upper limit of irritation at Sebastian Moncrieff.

Yet here she was, mere *hours* after their nocturnal encounter, seething at him with uncharacteristic vigor. Even in his absence he was a sliver beneath her skin.

An unrelenting prick.

She'd rolled like restless waves in the night, doing her best to escape fevered memories of the man. Recollections that became lurid dreams, once she'd finally wrestled sleep into submission.

Though morning had been her nemesis since she was a girl, Veronica was particularly fond of breakfast. Coffee and scones, biscuits and bacon, soft boiled eggs in their little cups, and toast drenched in butter. These were the things that beckoned her from the warmth of her bed each day.

And Sebastian Moncrieff, that arrogant bully, had deprived her of that pleasure this morning.

Had stolen it, like the knavish pirate he'd been.

That he apparently still *was*.

Because, though she was seated in one of Europe's most opulent first-class dining cars, sinking her teeth

18

into the butteriest croissant she'd had in ages, she could hardly taste a single morsel.

His scent had taken her olfactory senses hostage, filling her with the extraordinarily masculine flavors and aromas that were distinct to *him*. Warm, wild, and clean. Like bergamot and citrus...both sharpened and sweetened with notes of honey.

Should she bottle the essence, she'd make a bloody fortune.

*Damn* him for being free to walk the world she inhabited! For confining them into a space from which there was no escape. Were she to flee, she'd run out of track.

And even were she to leap from the train, he'd find her still.

She intrinsically knew that, somehow.

In her unbidden thoughts, she had often wondered if their paths would cross again. Of course, she'd always immediately rejected the idea. He'd been arrested by none other than Carlton Morley, the Chief Inspector at Scotland Yard. She'd watched as they'd led him away in irons.

Surely he'd have been tried for kidnapping, theft, privateering, even murder. As it was more than a year after his capture, he should have had his neck stretched by a rope.

Which was one of the reasons she avoided British papers. She found she didn't want to know. Because in all reality she *should* be relieved that justice had been done.

And yet...

A sudden cold dread clenched in her stomach, and she glanced across the table to see Penelope Weller's eyes widen in her elfin face with a brief flash of unmasked trepidation.

Veronica was horrifically, *intimately* acquainted with all that was hidden behind that very expression. The instant physical tension at the approach of an oppressor. The shattering of any pretense of inner peace. The anticipation of humiliation or condemnation. Of punishment and peril.

During her marriage to Mortimer Weatherstoke, the Earl of Southbourne, Veronica learned to read the most insignificant indications of emotion. Such as the tremble of Mrs. Adrienne Weller's teacup as she returned it to its saucer. The tight, compulsive movements of Penelope's throat as she worked to swallow her fear more than once. Hoping her voice wouldn't reveal the chaos within. The returning of both women's hands beneath the table, to grip at each other. To draw strength from a fellow captive.

Veronica steeled her own spine, measuring her voice and breath the moment before Arthur Weller joined them.

"And here I rushed to breakfast, beset with worry that your food would cool whilst you waited for me." He scowled down at his wife and daughter's breakfast plates, on which the food had been more poked and nibbled at than consumed. "I see I needn't have bothered."

This was how Weller expressed his disapproval. Sneering over the spectacles perching on his hawkish nose, he expelled the politest words from his mouth.

Yet they landed like a threat.

The subtext always being: *You will suffer for my displeasure.*

Men like him had so many vast and varied ways of collecting their dues. The range was incredibly wide, spanning from slight cuts and pinpricks of hurtful words, to physical blows that would beat a grown man into dust. Men like Arthur Weller didn't just break bones, he reached inside the people he should have protected and broke their spirits as well.

To say nothing of their hearts.

"I'm sorry, Papa," Penelope whispered, her gaze never leaving the table.

Because his wife and daughter could not speak up, Veronica did it for them, taking perverse pleasure in doing so.

Arthur Weller was always pleasant in public.

"Lend us your pardon, Mr. Weller, we were uncertain if you would join us this morning, as you did not yesterday." She kept her tone conversational, as if oblivious to the fraught atmosphere between the entire Weller family. "In fact, I didn't see you in your cabin at all, so it was assumed you'd awoken early and breakfasted already, seeing as how breakfast began a quarter hour past." Picking up a muffin, she slathered it with preserves and bit off an unladylike mouthful, chewing it *at* him.

This one tasted like strawberries and spite.

Veronica didn't have to look at him to recognize the wrath burning down at her from his dark eyes. Her attention remained firmly affixed to her food, not only because she didn't want to give Weller the satisfaction, but because she disliked the sight of him. He wasn't unsightly, *per se*. A wealth of silvering hair and an impressive mustache bracketed by muttonchops were affixed to rather mild features, weathered by his early years as a seaman. He'd kept that lean, rangy figure into his fifties, and stood taller than most men. Though he'd a volatile intensity about him that she'd noticed cowed people beneath him and his peers, alike. But he hadn't a build she would describe as intimidating.

Not when she'd stood in the presence of leviathans such as The Black Heart of Ben More and the Rook.

Of the tremendous titan that was Sebastian Moncrieff.

"How extraordinary you are, Countess," he replied in an indulgent tone. "Most women so devoted to fashion take care not to eat so much or so often. Though I suppose you are lucky to be possessed of the skills to let out your own gowns as the need, no doubt, arises."

Veronica offered him a smile she hoped did not bare as many teeth as she desired. "Dowager Countess," she corrected. "I know you were not educated with nobility, so I don't mind reminding you that it is commensurate to address me as 'my lady.'"

His eyes narrowed as his smile widened into something that would be accompanied by a snarl in the wild. "Ah yes, how very sad. You are often so jolly, I forget the man who lifted you out of the mire of mediocrity was murdered."

*And so shall you be.*

The savage thought astonished her.

Veronica was feeling less and less conflicted about his impending demise, and she'd only spent a matter of minutes in his company.

This man sold women and children, or so Moncrieff had mentioned. Just when she didn't think he could be any more evil...

Weller snapped his fingers at the staff and demanded his breakfast, cutting off any need for a reply. The Weller women didn't touch their food again until he'd received and dug into his own, and even then, they chewed as if the delicacies tasted of ash.

"I learned something from a...loquacious companion this morning," Weller said around a bite. He obviously referred to the mistress with which he'd spent the night, intending to embarrass or hurt his wife.

Men like him rarely realized that their absence was, in fact, a relief.

"You don't say, darling," Adrienne replied dutifully, batting her pale eyes at her husband in a most disarming way. She'd been a scandalously young bride, thereby possessed of an eligible daughter before her fortieth year. However, marriage to a man like Weller, and eight subsequent failed pregnancies, had pinched deep grooves into her forehead and bracketed her tight frown. Shadows haunted the skin beneath her eyes which sagged from exhaustion, and even her honey-colored coiffure seemed to droop in his presence.

Veronica remembered that self-same expression in the mirror.

Lord, but she wished she could take Adrienne with them, but like so many women she insisted on staying with her husband.

"What did you hear, Papa?" Penelope asked overbrightly, a white pinch encircling her smile and the skin on her knuckles as she stirred her tea.

He puffed out his chest. "Not only are the Duchess of Lowood and her daughter aboard, but also is the Erstwhile Earl. I met him in the observation car last night. Capital fellow, not at all like one hears in the papers."

Veronica froze.

*The Erstwhile Earl*. She'd heard that moniker before. When the Countess of Northwalk had mentioned it in regard to Sebastian Moncrieff.

Earl of Crosthwaite, she'd called him.

As tempted as Veronica had been to investigate the matter over the months since she'd encountered the man, she'd never allowed herself to do it.

To look into his past would be to admit that Moncrieff had a powerful effect on her, enough at least to arouse curiosity.

"Why do they call him the Erstwhile Earl?" she couldn't help but ask.

"Oh, you don't know?" A victorious chuckle washed her in revulsion. Men like Weller delighted in schooling the uninitiated. "Crosthwaite's father died when he was a lad away at boarding school. The title is old, granted back when a York held the throne, but old Henry Moncrieff lost the last of the fortune and began to parcel off the land to pay debts. Most everything else was taken in taxes upon his death. So, the boy never returned to the drafty ruin that even the Crown didn't want to bother with taking from him."

"He became a pirate, instead." Moncrieff's voice was as smooth, cold, and lethal as his blade from the night before.

Veronica nearly dropped her cup and was unable to avoid a slosh into the saucer as it landed with uncontrolled clatter.

Awareness poured down her spine, and every hair on her body vibrated at an alarming frequency. The electric sensations skittering through her threatened to set her aglow.

It was what his nearness always did to her.

She didn't turn to look, choosing instead to be completely absorbed by her breakfast plate. Yet, she knew exactly where he stood behind them, as if every nerve in her body recognized the proximity.

"My lord." Weller stood, wiping his mouth and turning to greet the Erstwhile Earl. "You'll forgive my idle gossip; I was regaling the ladies about your exploits. You're rather a legend."

"No forgiveness needed," came the amiable reply. "Though my deeds are hardly proper breakfast conversation."

Veronica witnessed his approach through Penelope

Weller's reaction. Her irises, dark like her father's, gave way to dilating pupils. Her pert nose flared, and her delicate jaw went slack as she arched her neck back, and then further, in order to take in the man's sheer immensity. A hand went to her hair, fluttering like a butterfly over the honey curls before smoothing over a lush green morning dress of Veronica's own creation.

Why did the girl have to look so comely in it? So young and unfettered?

Veronica blinked herself back to sanity.

*Why the devil did it matter?*

"Would you join us for breakfast?" Weller offered Moncrieff, snapping at a waiter and pointing at a chair he wanted taken from another table.

*Don't accept. Don't say yes,* Veronica pleaded inwardly. *Please just move along.*

"I've already dined," he answered, allowing her to expel her relief on a breath she hadn't known she'd been holding. "But how could I refuse at least one cup of tea with such lovely companions?"

*Drat and damn and blast!* She dug into her recollection of even more foul curses when the hem of his grey morning suit jacket found her periphery as he stepped to the table.

What in God's name was he doing? A man bent on murder should *not* be seen dining with his intended victim. How could he smile into Weller's face all the while expecting to slide a knife into him at the first appropriate moment?

"My lord, allow me to present my wife, Mrs. Adrienne Weller, and our daughter, Penelope." Arthur Weller swept a hand across the table as the women in question struggled to stand.

"Please, don't get up my account," was Moncrieff's pleasant reply. "I'll sit."

Weller made a grand gesture at Veronica who sat on his other side. "And this is the Dowager Countess Southbourne, the Paris fashion prodigy we've engaged to make Penny's wedding trousseau."

He loved to parade her in front of important people.

"My lord," she murmured in greeting. She could no longer avoid looking at him without drawing notice to her odd behavior, so she steeled her spine and lifted her gaze.

Instantly, she regretted it.

The shadows had been kind last night, concealing the full force of Sebastian Moncrieff's presence.

She'd forgotten he didn't belong to the darkness. That he was this lambent creature of almost blinding splendor, possessed of the depraved sort of good looks that one would ascribe to a pagan god of opulence and sensuality.

On a ship beneath the open, endless horizon he'd been an exceptionally large man.

But on a train where space was at a premium, he took too much of it for the comfort of regularly built people. Like Goliath, he was both a giant and a philistine.

With the scruples of a tomcat.

"A dowager countess employed by a shipping magnate?" Eyes the color of Brandywine lazily touched every part of her visible above the table. Veronica felt quite molested once he'd finished. "My how the world has changed in my years at sea."

Veronica's jaw went slack.

How casually he addressed his crimes. Wore his scandal on his skin and bared it to the world—nay, displayed it in pride of place, as if mischief and malice might be awarded a trophy.

A chair appeared behind him, and he rucked up his

trousers as he sat, making room for his powerful thighs. Dismissing Veronica, he turned the full weight of his charm toward Adrienne and Penelope. "I understand felicitations are in order on your impending nuptials, Miss Weller."

"T-thank you," the girl breathed, her cheeks staining a soft shade of pink.

It took nothing more than a slight smile in the direction of the staff to incite a parade of food and drink in an elegant dance performed only for men of his rank and power.

Ultimately, he ended up choosing an Irish breakfast tea, and pouring an offensive amount of cream and sugar into a cup that looked preposterously small in his hands. "Tell me, Miss Weller, who is the lucky groom?"

"A Count Gyürky in Bucharest," her father answered for her. "He's a direct descendant of Catherine the Great. Much like many of our own noble houses."

"A count, you say?" Belying his words, Moncrieff's sip of tea was decidedly unimpressed. "Ah, well...if you can't find nobility close by, it's worth looking abroad to the Continent."

"Yes—well—Gyürky's holdings are the size of Hampshire," Weller spluttered, not immune to the implied insult.

Veronica leveled Moncrieff with a scathing look, one he summarily ignored.

How abominably he was behaving. Did he not know that the pique coloring Weller's features would be felt by his family? That he'd take it out on the women as if his mortification were their fault?

"He's wealthier than so many of our impoverished noblemen," Weller said with a sniff.

"Yes, I'm certain his goats are well cared for," Moncrieff chuckled, then shrugged. "At least he's not an American."

"Or a *pirate*," Veronica said, finally drawing his notice.

"We were more privateers, my lady," he corrected with a solicitous smile, one that turned her insides rather slippery and soft. "Regardless of reputation, we generally pillaged according to the rules of maritime law."

"Generally?" Veronica wrinkled her nose and clenched her thighs. "Last I checked, the Royal Navy is not at war, nor was the Devil's Dirge under contract with the crown."

"Semantics." Moncrieff waved them away as if they held no bearing whatsoever. "It could be argued that any attack on a British vessel could be considered an act of war."

Was that how he'd wriggled out of trouble with the law?

Or was it because he'd turned the incomparable power of his pulchritude on the queen herself, and the besotted woman granted him full pardon?

*Un-bloody-believable.*

A handkerchief drifted on an invisible breeze, landing like a silken snowflake at Moncrieff's feet. It heralded the arrival of a strawberry-haired beauty, thrust into view by an older woman with similar features, but which drooped at the jaw like the jowls of a hound.

"Jessica, you are too clumsy," berated the matriarch, with overwrought affectation.

"Allow me." Sebastian bent in his chair and retrieved the scrap of fabric, offering it back to the girl, who was scarcely old enough to have been presented to society.

"Thank you," she demurred with a coy bat of her

lashes. "I'm ever so much obliged."

Obliged? He returned a scrap of fabric, not the stolen family jewels.

"Think nothing of it," he replied to the moon-eyed girl, whose entire face bloomed crimson at his wink.

"A true gentleman," the mother cooed from behind her daughter.

Veronica lowered her lashes to hide the complete orbit of her eyes. Surely, she couldn't be the only one to notice that all available debutantes seemed to be thanking him for his mere existence.

"Few who know me accuse me of being a gentleman, madam." His eyes glimmered with merriment as he took another measured sip of his tea.

"I see you don't recognize me," the elder woman addressed the table. "I am Heloise de Marchand, Duchess of Lowood."

This time, the assemblage stood with alacrity. One did not remain seated in the presence of a duchess until she gave her leave.

"Your Grace," Sebastian executed a perfect bow as the duchess nudged the girl forward with alarming blatancy.

"This is my daughter, Jessica."

"A pleasure, Lady Jessica." He caught the girl's forearm and slid his hand down until her gloved fingers curled over his as he bent to press a kiss over her knuckles.

Veronica's own hand curled, her nails biting into her palms.

"I am Sebastian Moncrieff, the Earl of—"

"We are well aware of you," the duchess interjected, as a woman of her age and standing was excused for lapses in manners, so long as they seemed to have done so on purpose. "One does not travel without knowing the importance of one's fellow passengers."

"Indeed." Sebastian flicked a glance at Weller. Or was it Veronica? They stood close enough in the cramped space it was impossible to tell. "Allow me, then, to make presentations to—"

"We've not the time, Moncrieff." The duchess sniffed toward the table, her only recognition of the existence of other people thus far. "Now that we've been introduced and you've proven yourself a gentleman, I'd like to invite you to our private car for breakfast."

His eyes lit with interest, and Veronica felt her own demeanor darken.

*He's a bloody pirate!* She wanted to scream. How could a woman—*a duchess*—be throwing her young, buxom daughter at the man? Did she not know his seat was in ruins? His family in shambles?

He'd been arrested only a year past!

"It would be rude to leave the lovely Wellers and the Dowager Countess Southbourne's company."

The duchess finally glanced over at them as if they were mud she'd scraped from the bottom of her shoe. "I'd have invited the Countess if she'd not regrettably returned to her origins in *trade*."

"Oh, I don't know," Moncrieff slid Veronica a speaking glance. "Fashion is more of a passionate hobby than anything. Much like the Duchess of Trenwyth does with her paintings."

Veronica's fingers itched to curl around his obscenely thick neck.

Opening her fan, the woman used it as a shield against the now awkward assembly. "The difference is vast, dear Moncrieff. The Duchess of Trenwyth's painting hangs in the Queen's own private quarters. She does not lease her services to *new money*."

New money. The phrase encompassed and oppressed the social standing of entrepreneurs such as manufacturers, transporters, and merchants who were quickly amassing fortunes, often far greater than those held by the landed lords.

Veronica couldn't see Weller's features, but his neck turned an alarming shade of purple.

"You are wicked," Moncrieff teased indulgently, though she noted that his smile was confined only to his lips. "Men like me are forced to dowry-hunt amongst new money, so I cannot share your sentiments."

The duchess's eyes glinted. "Follow me, Moncrieff, there's more to discuss on the topic of dowries." Her head gestured toward the door before she flared her skirts and sailed away, her diminutive daughter trailing in her wake.

Affecting a regretful expression, Moncrieff turned back to the table. "It seems noble duty calls." Rather than hurrying away, he bent and kissed the hand of each lady at the table, leaving Veronica for last. He reached across Weller to envelope her fingers, lips only hovering above her knuckles.

"It's been a rare pleasure," he said before sauntering away.

They all watched, mute, until he was forced to tilt his shoulders to the side in order to fit through the door.

"Insufferable man!" Weller threw his linen on the table and sat down in a heap. "I didn't like him from the moment I laid eyes on him," he said, as if he'd not been close to licking Moncrieff's boots only a moment before.

"I don't think he meant us disrespect," Penelope murmured, her voice painted with awe. "It's impossible to refuse a real-life duchess."

"Do you mean to disrespect me by defending him?" Weller snarled, his knuckles whitening as they gripped the side of the table.

Adrienne placed a hand on her daughter's shoulder, as the girl had gone several shades of green. "She meant nothing by it, Arthur. I'm certain we were all over-whelmed by our first brush with a woman of such rank and an earl of such...such..."

Weller leaned forward, his cheeks mottled with barely-leashed rage. "Such. *What*?" he asked from be-hind clenched teeth.

"Such infamy," she finished quickly.

His nostrils flared for a fraught moment, and then he leaned back into his chair, taking up his cutlery. "One wonders how a body would fare being thrown from a train at this speed," he speculated, apropos of nothing. "Do you think the snow would cushion a fall?"

Veronica didn't remark on the ill-concealed threat, directed at no one in particular. Her entire being was focused on the piece of rolled-up paper Moncrieff had tucked into her hand.

## Four

Sebastian . . .

**SEBASTIAN** most often found anticipation a
delicious form of torture.

However, that was before he'd had to wait in the
third cargo car back from second class, wondering if
Veronica Weatherstoke would be the first woman in his
personal history to deny an invitation to meet him.

Rather than luggage, his surroundings were dedi-
cated to freight and shipped goods of every imaginable
kind. Copper pipes lashed to the right wall gleamed in
the wan light from the window. Across from them,
bolted shelves propped up gluttonous bags of barley and
seed. Crates of frozen butter were stacked neatly by
fragile boxes of wine glasses.

There *would* be a battalion of wine glasses. Their
next stop was Paris, after all.

When the far door opened, he breathed a sigh of relief and flattened his back to the wall, hoping the shelves
and shadows would provide him cover.

Veronica swept in and turned instantly to lock the
door against the winter wind, before glancing at the
gloom of the interior. Her attentions were immediately
diverted by a tightly packed pile of worn furniture.

Chairs with torn velvet upholstery were stacked upon three-legged tables and the corpses of armoires, all secured by leather straps and chains.

As she'd not yet alerted to his presence, Sebastion took the opportunity to observe her in an artless, uninhibited moment. She inspected every piece of abused antiqued furniture as she pulled her peach gloves from each individual finger.

Why he found the action unbearably erotic, he couldn't say.

It was bloody cold in these unheated cargo cars, why would she be taking off her gloves?

Oh... Oh fuck.

Questioning fingertips entranced him as they tested the textures and details of several pieces while thoughts and opinions escaped her throat in slight speculative sounds. A wordless murmur of discovery, a crestfallen sigh, a small *oh* of surprise as she discovered something unexpected.

He'd been a fool to suggest they meet in such confines, though he did note that it was safer than anywhere with a bed.

Not that he'd ever needed a bed to enjoy sex. Any surface would do, really.

Carefully, almost reverently, Veronica stroked the scratched, pocked surface of a desk, her fingers finding the grooves and following them to their fruition. Closing her eyes, she indulged in a private moment, as if she shared a memory with the desk that caused her to gain three shades of peach to her cheeks.

Sebastian had flirted with, fondled, and fucked an untold number of beautiful women. He was a hedonist at heart, and did his utmost to live up to his reputation at every turn. A man driven by desire, by the indulgence thereof, he consumed whatever pleasure a moment could provide, stretching it out to the final drop.

In the bacchanalia that had been his life, he couldn't ever remember wanting a woman with such ardency.

Truly, it bordered on violence.

Not violence *toward* her, so much as a ferocious, primitive reaction slamming into his body with the power of a war hammer. Skewering him with wicked lances of lust before mocking him with her indifference.

Not only did this leave him intensely perturbed, but also uncharacteristically perplexed. Though painfully ardent, this was no rutting need to throw his hips forward into a warm orifice with a pretty face.

His hands itched to build things for her. To break what insulted her. He wished for a bullet to throw his body in front of. Or a tyrant to topple in her name.

These almost sophomoric desires and drives hadn't been a part of his intentions toward women since he was a lad of fourteen, desperate for a dragon to slay to win his damsel.

As a man, he'd become the monster.

Still was, in her eyes.

Driven by an intensifying inquisitiveness, he crept forward, no longer hiding himself, but also not calling attention to his presence.

Something about the old desk had absorbed her notice so thoroughly, he'd moved close enough to reach for her and she'd yet to register that she was not alone.

He adopted a sprightly tone, so as not to startle her overmuch. "What a lovely old piece. I was fond of one very much like it in my quarters on the Devil's Dirge."

Veronica whirled toward him, pulling her hand away from the surface of the desk as if it'd burned her.

"How did you get in here?" she demanded breathlessly.

35

"Same door as you."

"You mean...you've been here all along?" Her winged, ebony brows met in a scowl. "You did not announce yourself upon my arrival."

"I hope you can forgive my wickedness," he murmured, thinking of all the multitudes of meaning that statement could convey. "It is only that you swept into the gloom looking like a Caribbean sunrise, and I was too breathless to greet you."

Her wary gaze had yet to meet his, and he was getting the idea she found his flirting more aggravating than amusing. His compliment did not go entirely unappreciated, he noted, as she smoothed an idle hand down her bodice and scrutinized the drapes of her lovely skirt before tugging at them.

"What do you want with me?" she inquired of the ground with no little amount of impatience. "Because of your shameful behavior today, I'm keen to stay close to Penelope and Adrienne as Arthur Weller is now in a rotten mood and likely to take it out on them."

"I've been told Weller is in the casino car with his young mistress...the Weller women are safe from his moods for the moment."

"Excellent," she clipped, reaching out to pick at a sliver from the edge of the desk. "I don't want to keep you from courting the duchess's daughter, so if you'll just state your business, I'll be on my way."

His lips twisted into a grimace at the thought of the vapid lady Jessica and her militant mother. "They're courting me, more like. I'd rather leash my life to a leathered old sow."

"Even with her excessive dowry?" she asked, lifting a skeptical brow.

"You forget, my lady, that I've a pirate's hoard of treasure, and no one's whim but my own to spend it on.

I need a debutant's dowry like the lake district needs more rain."

"Oh." She blinked rapidly. "But I've been told your estate and finances are in ruin."

"Come now, Countess, do you believe everything the gossip mill has to offer? Besides, why restore a defunct ruin when I could spend my ill-gotten gains on myself rather than a legacy I'm not likely to sire."

Though his response seemed to trouble her, she still refused to lift her eyes above his cravat. "I suppose your answer in that regard shouldn't surprise me. So, if you please, would you tell me why you've summoned me, and we can both return to the business of the day."

"That very business is why I'd like to speak with you," he said. "I awoke curious as to exactly how you plan to spirit poor Penelope and her lover to America. And also to offer my assistance, such as it is."

"Why would you do that?" she asked suspiciously.

Because Arthur Weller was a dangerous man to cross. Because the conscience he thought he'd buried whispered that her broken trust in him was a fault he needed to work to regain. *Because* something about her overrode every selfish instinct he'd carefully cultivated over the decades.

He could say none of this out loud.

"Because, dear lady, I cannot do my part until yours is done, and impatience is chief among my vast assortment of flaws."

"I see." His answer seemed to mollify her. "Well, the plan is a simple one, really. Once we pull into Gare de Lyon, I've a contact that will conduct us in his coach to Le Havre where they're booked on a steamship to America under pseudonyms."

"I'm impressed." Sebastian examined her with different eyes. She was so shrewd for someone so gentle. A ruthless mind did not often maintain such a soft heart, encased in all that exquisite loveliness.

Lord but she transfixed him.

"You said 'us' when discussing the journey to Le Havre. Does that mean you're going with them?"

"Yes."

The idea of such distance curdled like bad cream in his gut. "To America?"

"No, to the ship. I want to see them off safely, but I also want to come back for Adrienne. She doesn't know that she'll be alone in this world once her husband and only child are gone."

"What if Weller does something to subvert this elopement?" he asked. "Do you have contingencies?"

"Of course." She rolled her eyes, crossing defensive arms over her chest, doing lovely things to her decolletage. "It will be night when we pull into Paris, so in the unlikely event that Arthur Weller disengages himself from his mistress to prevent us from leaving the train, I suppose I'll just have to create a diversion."

"That, at least, will be simple, as I'm certain you're aware you're one of the most diverting creatures on the planet." He reached toward a wayward ringlet that'd come loose from her coiffure and fallen in front of her eyes.

She jerked her head back before he could touch her and retreated several steps. "Please don't."

His hand froze mid-air. Several dark suspicions swirled about in his chest, ones that condemned all those of his sex into a lake of eternal hellfire. A fire he'd often the mind to stoke himself. "Veronica, why can you not look at me?"

"I *am* looking at you."

"My throat does not count. Look at *me*."

Her brows knit together, and even in the dimness

her cheeks flared a color vibrant enough to rival her dress. "Do not presume to tell me where to look or what to do, sir. You are not my keeper nor my master."

"On the contrary, my lady," he murmured. "I am but your humble servant."

Her gaze latched onto the desk against which his hip now rested. "Are we finished? Or was there something else to discuss?"

"Something has driven you to a pique," he observed. "Was it Weller?"

"It was not."

"Was it me?"

Her silence answered for her as she scratched at a wound in the wooden desktop.

As much as he desired it, he made no move to go closer to her. "Do I frighten you?"

She scoffed. "Not in the least."

*Lie.*

"Come now, I know I've been a cad and a rogue the whole of my life, but are you really afraid that I'll hurt you?" He held his hands out, offering himself up for scrutiny. Surely a woman with your fashion sense would deduce that a man with such a light-grey suit wasn't planning on getting any blood on it. And the fit of it didn't at all allow for tight maneuvering— he'd split the seams.

"You're a criminal and confessed pirate, Moncrieff," she stated with a droll huff. "Your crew was rather famous for hurting people."

"Never women," he asserted, holding up his finger to make the salient point. "It was a veritable creed of ours that women and children would always be spared much possible distress from our pirating. One of Rook's sticking points, with which I heartily agreed. You and

Lorelai were among the first ladies to ever board the ship."

To his utter astonishment, she snorted. "You are a filthy liar."

"Uncalled for," he admonished her without letting his good nature slip. "How do you figure?"

She gaped at him as if he were the largest, dimmest bulb she'd ever had to contend with. "Our second night on that ship, the captain brought a veritable contingent of prostitutes to entertain the entire crew."

Laughing that away, he waved his hand at her. "That doesn't count—our anchor was down."

"Gah!" She threw her arms up and shifted as if she wanted to pace the length of the aisle. "You are the most ridiculous, infuriating man. How you avoided the noose is one of the great mysteries of our time."

"It really isn't." He chuckled, enjoying how lovely aggravation made her, even in the pallid, grey light of winter filtered through the grime of the window. "I was given an ultimatum, of sorts. It was either declare myself the Erstwhile Earl of Crosthwaite, take up my political seat and lordly responsibilities...or prison, and likely the noose. I will tell you it was one of the most difficult decisions I've yet made. The life of a lord is tedious in the extreme. There are days I would have preferred the gallows."

A noise, half disbelief, half frustration, burst from her chest. "This is why everyone hates the aristocracy."

"Says the countess."

"Dowager!" she cried. "And I never *asked* to be a countess, I fell for Mortimer Weatherstoke before I knew he was an earl's son."

Now it was his turn to be incensed. "If you tell me you loved that cretinous bastard, I'll pitch myself from the train right now."

"Tempting as that outcome may be, I cannot claim to have loved Mortimer Weatherstoke. I found him charming whilst we courted. He was one of the handsomest men I'd met in society, and never revealed the rot he'd festering in his soul until it was too late."

Questions crowded into Sebastian's throat until they choked him into silence. He wanted to understand her damage. To not merely patch up the holes perforating her soul and spirit...but to truly mend them.

*How can someone as broken as you fix her?* queried his conscience. *She is better than you will ever be.*

This whisper was precisely why he'd locked his cursed conscience away some time ago, and never planned to set it free again.

What fucking key did this woman hold to spring his better self from its carefully maintained prison?

"I did not desire a title," she continued. "I wanted to be a wife. To bring my family pride. To care for a grand home and devote myself to various philanthropic causes. I wanted to raise kind sons and strong daughters. I wanted... Why are you looking at me like that?"

"Because I'm going to kiss you," he blurted. "I thought that was bloody obvious."

"You are *not*."

Except...she didn't step back this time.

"You want me to."

Her luscious mouth dropped open. "I *never*."

*Gigantic. Lie.*

"And why not?" he asked, mindful of the fact that many people lied to themselves, most of all. Especially when it came to affairs of the heart.

Or any affairs, really.

Her eyes lifted above his tie, for once, but stalled on his lips. "I know where that mouth has been." She made a disgusted face.

"As they've always been attached to my face," he teased, "I can vouch for their whereabouts exclusively. I vow they've never ventured where they ought not."

"I know they've found their way between the thighs of a common strumpet," she accused. "They could be diseased."

"Have they?" He scratched his head, thoroughly enjoying himself. So, the countess was a gossip? What fun —he'd found a delightful flaw they could share. "There are simply too many strumpets to remember them all, though I'm not at all in the habit of paying for anything considered common."

"How could you forget?" She threw her hands up in the air as if giving up. "You were feasting—nay —*fiending* on her that day in the ship. I thought you might be in danger of losing your tongue in her—"

"You. Watched?" Every muscle in Sebastian's body clenched at the very idea. Not with anger or embarrassment, no, with something much more dangerous than that. Suddenly his desire had teeth and claws, ripping his skin and his uncultivated self-discipline to shreds.

Luckily, she was too irked to notice. "I was looking for an escape! I certainly didn't install that lens between your stateroom and my prison."

"It was hardly a prison," he defended. "That bedroom boasted the most comfortable mattress on the entire ship. The crystal alone cost—"

"The door locked from the outside!"

"Only to keep you from doing yourself a mischief. You were threatening to leap into the ocean in the middle of a storm to attempt an impossible swim back to shore."

"To avoid a fate as offensive as that poor prostitute had to suffer beneath *you*."

Sebastian remembered the encounter, because he'd

been so inflamed by the woman in the next room, he'd selected a strumpet with similar hair and blazing green eyes. He'd feasted upon her, and then he'd filled her every orifice with the singular enthusiasm he'd felt toward this particular prisoner.

He'd watched the wall that separated him as he'd come, not knowing that she was pressed to the very oculus they used to keep an eye on their captives.

Watching him in return.

He'd be damned if that didn't send every available drop of blood straight to his cock.

Luckily, he'd spent twenty years learning to layer indifference over any other emotion as he interacted with the world. "As a point of clarification, I wonder just what about my performance offended you so?"

"The entire bloody thing offended me," she exclaimed. "From start to—to—finish."

*I've got you*, he thought, unfurling the smile of a Cheshire cat.

"One must wonder, my lady, if you found what you saw as offensive as you claim, then why watch the entire display?"

It was cruel, really, to remain silent while she sputtered and groped for an answer she likely didn't understand. But the discovery was too delicious not to dine on for a few moments before taking pity on her. "There's nothing to be ashamed of, Countess, we've all a bit of a voyeur inside of us...some more than others, apparently."

"I am *not*—"

"I've a point of contention, however." He held up a finger. "At no time was that woman—or any woman of my intimate acquaintance, for that matter—in a state of suffering. Were you watching closely, you'll notice I pleasured her to fruition at least twice before allowing my own. That is a personal point of pride for me."

Wrapping her arms around her middle in a decidedly protective gesture, the Veronica still didn't cave to his excellent point. "Women like her are paid to stroke the ego of a man. They can manufacture their pleasure as well as any wife."

He did not miss her inadvertent admission there, but smoothly avoided picking at it. "I've paid a woman to stroke many parts of me, madam, but my ego has never been in need."

"Now *that* I believe," she said acerbically. "Though I suppose your overinflated sense of self would not allow you to imagine that a woman might have faked her enjoyment of your attentions."

"Never happened."

"So, say you all," she challenged. "But I know there are ways to manufacture one's enjoyment to appear like the real thing."

"Certainly," he agreed. "But there are ways to tell, so many men ignore it, either because of ignorance or simple selfishness. These are impossible to fabricate."

"If you say so."

"If a man is simply searching for writhing yips, then he could certainly be fooled," Sebastian conceded, lowering his voice and leaning toward her. "But, like so many untamed creatures, a woman's desire is so often conveyed with unspoken, incontrollable signals. Take, for example, the dilation of her eyes. The plumping of her lips with blood and the tightening of her nipples. Her breath will come more quickly, and her delicate nostrils will flare."

Sebastian very much enjoyed the fact that she did her level best to measure her rapid breaths and tuck her full lips against her teeth.

"The same could be said of a frightened woman, as an aroused one," she said, in a voice husked with sensation and tightened with strain.

"If I cannot tell from a woman's reaction if she is aroused, then it is indisputable that her sex will reveal all."

"You're...you're being absurd," she accused.

If he reached out and touched her cheek in that moment, Sebastian might have diagnosed her with a fever. She was ripe and primed, and that likely contributed to her temper.

A gentleman would allow her a moment to recover.

But he never claimed to be a gentleman, and the predator within him could scent her arousal like a shark sensed blood in the water.

Now was no time for a retreat.

Instead, he splayed his hand close to hers on the desk and leaned down until his lips hovered above the shell of her ear. Not one part of them touched the other.

But every nerve in his body was alive with the feel of her. Attuned to the very vibrations of her atmosphere. "Your intimate skin flushes with color," he continued, in a voice barely above a whisper, threatening to be swept away by the rhythmic cacophony of the train. "The hood of delicate flesh becomes swollen, engorged, revealing the clever, magical button it protects. That delicious little place where so much of your pleasure is contained. The folds will be slippery with desire, and if paid the correct attention, you'll release a flood of moisture upon your climax that would take me two swallows to contain. Your muscles would clench at my cock with powerful, chaotic little spasms. Trust me, my beauty, these are things that cannot be feigned. Surely you know that."

She said nothing. *Did* nothing.

In fact, they stood like that for so long he straightened and pulled away to examine her with a twinge of concern.

"*Do* you know that? Have you ever…"

She stared down at their fingertips splayed on the desk, as close as they could be without touching. Breath sawed in and out of her with marked difficulty, unsteady with the force of her trembles.

These were no small vibrations, Sebastian noted. But great, bone-wracking tremors, wrought by overpowering emotion.

He knew the answer, and the heart he claimed to have left on some deserted island somewhere broke at the injustice.

"Veronica. Look at me."

She flinched, but didn't retreat. Perhaps he was being unintentionally crueler than he realized. He wanted to torment her with arousal. But…what if arousal was a torment for her?

What if Mortimer Weatherstoke created wounds that were still taking time to scar?

Swallowing a surge of rage, he slid his hand closer, allowing the energy to arc between them before the pads of their fingers touched.

"Look at me," he pressed, gentler this time.

With infinite slowness, she tilted her neck back until their gazes met and held. Even in the dim light, her eyes gleamed the color of the most exotic eastern jade.

To Sebastian's astonishment, something within him calmed.

In the past, he'd been told that to look into the eyes of the right woman was like falling, losing oneself in their color, or perhaps drowning in their depths. The earth would move, the planets would align, and all that melodramatic, romantical nonsense.

How intriguing to learn they'd been wrong.

This was neither falling nor drowning. Quite the opposite, in fact.

The earth had ceased to move entirely.

For once in his bedeviled life, Sebastian quieted. He stilled. Cords of velvet and silk encircled his limbs and secured him to this spot, to this moment, forcing him to remain in one place long enough to catch up with himself...

And take a breath.

A slow, easy inhale, flavored with notes of orchid and amber, bloomed inside of his chest with the languid deliberation of a sunset. Refusing to bend to the will of Man, God, or the relentless influence of Time itself, the sensation struck him dumb and stripped him of the wits upon which he so heavily relied.

Miraculous.

There was no other word for it. With each breath taken deeper into his chest, the consistent tightness eased, replaced by another need that surprised him as precious little did in this world.

His desire, though all-consuming, had lost its violent edge. The possession and provocation thrumming through his veins paused in his chest to expand and melt, before flowing in languid, honeyed beats to the rest of him, carrying a foreign substance as dangerous as any toxin.

One to which he couldn't subscribe an exact identification.

Tenderness, perhaps. Vulnerability. Need, in its most generous form.

The need to worship the parts she kept hidden, even from herself. To adore what had never even been appreciated. To give to her what had only been taken.

He knew the bliss of unrepentant indulgence. He'd

tasted the sweetness of discarded inhibitions. He'd drenched himself in pleasure so heady it'd bled into pain and become all the more intense for it.

And this vision of desire had never even been allowed a taste?

In-fucking-tolerable.

"Veronica." Lord how he loved to say her name. How he hoped he could whisper it against her sex. "Let me make you come."

# *Five*

"I AM *NOT* HAVING sex with you." It wasn't a sentence Veronica imagined she'd be forced to utter today.

Or ever.

Especially not to this man.

Furthermore, she'd never even considered that the denial would be a difficulty.

Sebastian Moncrieff had her pinned down. Not physically, but in every other conceivable way. Somehow, he'd guessed at the desire she'd discovered more than a year ago, as she'd witnessed him fornicate with another woman.

On a desk very much like this one.

His head had danced between the woman's thighs, and drawn by a macabre curiosity, Veronica had watched in fascination as the woman had cried and strained and screamed beneath his attentions.

Veronica's disbelief had been accompanied by another distressing discovery. One that'd made her thighs clench on an aching pulse accompanied by a yawning chasm of emptiness deep in her womb.

The sight of his naked body had intensified the

ache. The play of muscle swelling and cording in his arms and shoulders. The flat of his tongue on forbidden flesh. The strain of his taut abdominals as he hammered her into the desk.

It was the first time she'd watched a woman climax. That she'd known such a thing was possible.

Her body had responded by releasing a rush of wet desire, and the ache had been so overwhelming that even the friction of her thighs with each step was impossibly, *unbearably* sensual against the slick thrum of need.

She'd resisted him then, and hadn't had to contend with such unwanted sensations in the time since.

Until today, when he insisted upon invoking the wicked memories, along with her body's reaction to them.

He'd explained her own desire to her, which should be the most aggravating factor in the entire world.

And yet, here she was, a pulsing puddle of slick arousal, her legs ready to give out at any moment.

She refused to give him the satisfaction.

"I'm never doing *that* again," she vowed. "I know you think you are some legendary sort of lover, and I'm sure you've honed your skills with untold multitudes of women, but I will not yield. You can look to take your pleasure elsewhere—am I understood?"

Closing her eyes, she wished her voice carried the same strength as did the words, but alas, her voice trembled as pathetically as her legs did.

"I think it is I who am misunderstood by you, dear Veronica," he said. "I'm not after taking pleasure, only giving it."

She did her level best to wither him with a look. "I have not given you leave to address me so informally. It is 'my lady' or nothing at all." She wasn't the sort that insisted on such proprieties, except when her hackles were so thoroughly engaged. She needed space. Air. A moment to think! All of which was in short supply in his presence.

"Seeing as we're contriving a murder together, I reckoned we were past such distinctions."

"Well..." She groped about for a witty rejoinder and came up with exactly nothing. "We're not. It is just such distinctions that keep us civil."

"Fine—then allow me a kiss, my lady?"

She eyed him warily, unstitched by the dimples beneath his puckish smile. By the width of his jaw and the roguish sparkle in his otherwise lethal eyes. He was the embodiment of carnality. Temptation incarnate sent from the Devil himself, to entice her.

"Only a kiss?" What was she doing? Surely not considering this madness. "You'll expect no...no pleasure from me?"

You have my word."

"Words are empty," she said on a hitch of breath as he lifted a finger to her lips, tracing whisper soft trails of fire on the outline of her mouth.

"One finger." That finger traced down her chin, the tiny buttons of her high-necked gown, down the center of her throat, awakening nerve endings she was unaware she'd possessed. "And a kiss. That's all I ask. If I touch you with anything else, you have my permission to cut the offending appendage off."

Curiosity overcame her contrariness. "One finger?"

"So long as it has free rein to roam where it likes."

Intimate muscles gave an involuntary clench. "I don't know..."

"It is a proposal of zero risk, my lady, with only pleasure to be gained. To be guaranteed."

"But what if..." She paused, a familiar insecurity gripping her.

Mortimer had always been angered at her lack of response, her grimaces of pain, and her general discomfort in the marriage bed. He'd humiliated her in front of doctors and mocked her openly about her frigidity. After so long, she'd been beyond caring what disappointed the brute, let alone what pleased him.

But this man? Something told her she would not withstand his disdain. Could not risk it.

"What if I am not able?" she whispered.

A storm gathered on his features that somehow made him all the more beautiful. "Woman, during this impossible and purely hypothetical event, the fault would entirely be mine. I would have failed us both and would immediately request another attempt."

*It wouldn't be her fault.*

None of this was her idea, responsibility, nor was it incumbent upon her to even perform her duty of *receiving* the pleasure...

How many nights had she lain awake, beset with the memory of that woman writhing beneath him? How many times had she wondered? Wanted? Yearned?

For a mere taste of what he did to her.

"One finger," she acquiesced.

The splendor of his victorious smile blinded her, and it took an embarrassingly long time for her to figure out just why he patted the top of the desk. "I would help you climb up, but alas even *my* finger is not so strong."

She opened her mouth to verbally protest, while her body moved to comply, sliding onto the desktop until her feet swung above the floor.

Eyes gleaming like a predator who only stalked at night, his mouth descended, claiming hers before she could change her mind.

## IT WAS JUST AS WELL.

His kiss melted away any objection with a suffusion of instantaneous warmth. In contrast, his lips were cool and dry as they swept and slanted across her stunned mouth, quietly unraveling every knot of her taut, anxious muscles. She'd expected passion from him—skillful, artful seduction, and dominant, masculine impatience.

What she found instead was a coaxing, tender exploration. Unhurried and uncomplicated. Even though he carefully held his tremendous body away from her own, he somehow imprinted upon every inch of her.

And yet...she was not distracted by roaming hands or the fervent press of his demanding arousal.

Her entire being was focused on the firm, shifting pressure of his mouth as he nibbled at the corners of her own before exerting the tiniest sucking tension, pulling her passion-plumped bottom lip to roll between his.

Lord but it was lovely and—*oh!*

A velvet swipe of his tongue against the seam of her mouth stole all breath from her body and all the thoughts from her head.

She lost herself in the seductive heat of this act. So familiar to a woman once married, and yet so foreign. This man was different in every way to her husband.

The shape of him, the scents and sentiments.

The safety.

That word gave her a moment's pause. This man exuded danger. Radiated wicked disregard for all things reliable and reasonable.

For heaven's sake, he was there to murder a man.

So why did she suddenly want to enfold herself against him? To crawl into his arms like a child and make a cradle of his strength...

When his seeking tongue once again tested the topography of her mouth, she opened for him with a sibilant sigh, before fully realizing what she'd done.

Alarmed, she braced herself for the invasion. The wet, smothering plunge that would create a mash of lips against teeth and a gagging sort of fullness in her throat.

She nearly expired when he met her own tongue with his before retreating, testing the curve of her lips as he did. That soft sucking motion invited her tongue into his mouth, enticing her to explore the warmth there.

He tasted divine.

Both bitter and sweet, like the finest, darkest chocolate. He made way for her exploration while caressing and teasing her with silky darts and swirls. It was not a dance to which she knew the steps, but he led her with a precision and expertise she relied upon.

Hollow, guttural noises and deep, appreciative sounds encouraged her on, vibrating across her lips, into her mouth, and down her spine to land at the very core of her desire.

So absorbed was she in the kiss—the first kiss that truly curled her toes—she'd been oblivious to his other designs until cold air kissed the tender skin above her stockings.

Ripping her mouth from his with a gasp, she clutched at the pile of skirts he'd gathered above her knees.

"Yes, do secure them there, that will be ever so helpful," he urged with a playful tone, though something both savage and devious glinted in his eyes.

"This isn't—what the devil are you—I don't think we—"

He pressed that infernal finger to her lips. "Now is not the time to think, Countess, but to *feel*."

Hot breaths exploded around the flat of his finger and arrested his gaze, while she trembled and struggled with her desires, her past, and her crippling anxieties. "I don't know what I feel," she confessed, unable to keep the wobble from her chin. "I don't know how to feel. How to do any of this in the way that—"

He smoothed the back of his knuckle over her chin, hooking the finger beneath it to lift her face to meet his.

"Do nothing," he said firmly.

She shook her head, but he didn't release her. "I don't understand."

"I've a delightful task to perform. However, *your* entire—and might I say delectable—body has but one job. To think and do as little as is possible. Do not feel on my account, only yours. Don't go looking for pleasure, let it find you."

"But—"

"Do your best to resist me, to remain unaffected. Do nothing at all, if you are so inclined."

"But then you won't be able to make me—"

His hand left her mouth and stole its way beneath her skirts. The fingertip traced the seams of her stockings against her thigh robbing her of the ability to speak. To breathe.

"Doubt me all you dare," he said darkly against her lips. "But do not rush your satisfaction, my lady. I am eager for the challenge."

He stole what was left of her sanity with another kiss, this one more ardent and impassioned than before. It drew from her a surprising form of impatience as he unleashed the full force of his seductive prowess upon her unsuspecting, insignificant defenses.

A spin of his tongue accompanied the rasp of his rough finger against the edge of her stockings. A barely-there nip of his teeth drew her attention from the line he traced up her thigh.

When he found the seam of her drawers, she couldn't tell which of them uttered the deep, needy moan. Though he was gentle and methodical, she could still sense the pace of his heart, hammering with a rhythm as furious as her own.

And then he was *there*.

One finger, true to his word, stroking through intimate hair and delving into soft, wet flesh.

She liquified beneath his touch, her legs melting further apart, her pulse abandoning its vocation and her lungs emptying of breath. She needed none of it to survive...

Not when the slippery warmth of his hand suffused her with such electric sensation.

With life.

Crooning soft, unintelligible words against her skin between worshipful little kisses, he smoothed his lips over her hairline, her eyes, her nose, her chin, and her cheekbones before dragging his mouth down the sensitized curve of her jaw, igniting erotic sparks of sensation over her entire body.

His leisurely explorations through engorged ruffles of her feminine sex was a turbulent lesson in frustration. Not only had her anxieties fled, she was instantly overtaken by a demanding urgency.

One he apparently seemed inclined to ignore.

"Dear God, but I could do this all day," he groaned against her ear. "You are so sweet, so slick, so abidingly perfect."

She couldn't summon the words to reply. Not only because of what his diabolical finger was doing to her, but because of the deliberate depth of his voice. The gratification she identified in the words and the fervency of his tone.

It was suddenly as if someone else had taken control of her body. For surely, *she* would not undulate her spine forward, rolling her hips against his finger, seeking the one touch that he couldn't seem to give her. She was not the sort of woman who squirmed and gasped in wordless, artless physical pleas.

It was only that the aggravating man had touted his skills so adroitly, and all he seemed to be able to do is build some sort of throbbing, arching, aching, almost painful pressure to a fevered pitch.

Sweat bloomed on her body and her spine cracked with her next demanding arch.

"Why?" the question ripped from her dry throat.

He lifted his mouth from her throat. "Why what, my darling?"

"Why won't you just..." She had no idea what he needed to do. To move, to find that place that throbbed and release it before she screamed.

"Oh, my poor lady, I am being exceedingly cruel. Selfish even."

"Why?" she whispered again, hating him a little. Wanting him a lot. Needing him more than she liked to admit. Craving what he was doing to her. Among other things.

"Because I didn't think that you'd come apart so easily...so quickly. I hoped to play for longer..." Upon a reluctant sigh, his clever finger did something that made her entire body jerk before pulling back.

Play? Was this recreation for him? When he was so obviously not the focus of the game, but the arbiter of it... How could he be enjoying it so much?

She rolled her hips in a display beyond the reach of shame. "Please." The plea escaped on a desperate sound, closer to a whine than she cared to admit.

"This is why you are dangerous," he growled, as if to himself. "No matter what I want, it seems I am powerless to deny you anything."

With that, he unleashed an erotic assault upon her sex that appropriated what was left of her dignity. Carnal strokes evoked torturous shivers that built upon themselves until they coalesced into clenching pulses. She cried out. Her arms reaching for him, clutching at his shoulders with helpless claws as wave after wave of unencumbered ecstasy threatened to drag her out into an ocean of lust and languor. Just when she thought the moment might pass, it escalated into another thrilling, soul-searing burst until the sensation became so exquisite, she could no longer distinguish the difference between pleasure and pain.

When she began to writhe, to seek escape, the pressure of his finger lifted but did not leave her. He let her down slowly, bringing her back from the brink and allowing her to float upon the smaller waves as they pushed her back toward the shore.

When she returned to herself, bedraggled and half-drowned, Veronica realized that Sebastian had kept his word. He'd not touched her with aught but his mouth and one finger.

One magical, maniacal finger.

She, however, had attached herself to the thick column of his body as if he were the only thing keeping her from being swept away and lost.

Realizing that she was clinging to him like a ridiculous ninny, she disentangled herself from him, suddenly tentative and shy.

His arms moved, as if to hold her in place, but he stopped short of touching her.

"My God." If she had to ascribe a word to his tone, it would be *marvel*. "I've been to every place claiming to be a wonder in this world. I've handled treasure you wouldn't believe existed. I've toured galleries and museums with the greats, names you would expire to hear. And never in this lifetime have I witnessed anything so beautiful as your body arched in climax."

A strangled giggle escaped her, and she placed a hand on his chest to halt the kiss he intended for her lips. "You needn't flatter me," she assured him.

He made a wry sound. "I have never flattered you, Countess. Were I a sculptor, I'd recreate it so you could agree with me. But, alas, I was born without talent in that regard."

She couldn't be so certain of that. She'd been nothing more than a boneless, shapeless heap in his hands, and with untold skill he'd...

Well, he'd transformed her.

The realization was a bitter one. She didn't want something so irrelevant to him as a passing tryst in a dusty cargo car to be a formative moment in her life.

But here she was, adrift in a storm of her own making.

Up until now, her entire existence had been about

what she could do for others. How she appeared to them. She'd been so aware of her every movement, what her features conveyed, how to modulate her voice and moderate her words in just such a way. She'd been the creation of her social-climbing parents, her finishing school, the rigorous life of a countess, and ultimately the quick temper and heavy fists of her husband.

For one surreal encounter, Sebastian Moncrieff had stolen that capability.

No, she was being unfair.

He'd *relieved* her of that *obligation*. Had converted her into a creature of need and hunger and unfettered pleasure. A pleasure he'd offered. Gifted. Without so much as a whisper of *quid pro quo*.

What kind of man did such a thing? Here she thought she had his measure. That she'd peeked into his empty heart and found it beat only at his pleasure.

Was there more to the Erstwhile Earl than even he realized?

Pulling back, she arched her neck to look up at him.

The taut mien of his skin pulled across hungry bones made him look older and even more dangerous. His gaze was feral and greedy, his jaw hard.

When his lips parted, fear lanced through her, turning her pulse to thunder.

The Devil was about to demand his due. What would he do to her if she refused?

"Let me use my mouth. I could coax another from you if you'd let me."

She blinked. Once. Again. Uncertain she heard him correctly. He wanted to give *her* another climax. With his mouth?

Unbidden, her eyes traversed the length of his body to find the barrel of his erection straining the front of his trousers.

Lord but he was large.

"Don't." The snarl rumbled from deeper in his chest than she dared to venture. "Don't look at me like that. Don't touch me or I—" He cut off, taking a long moment to compose himself. "Just let me taste you?"

"I can't." Her tight throat worked over a swallow. "I can't right now."

"Oh, trust me, Countess, you can."

"No. I mean..." She struggled with her skirts, shoving them back over her knees and sitting straight. "I have to go to Penelope. There is too much to do... Weller could be returning for them."

He pushed himself away from the desk with a tortured groan. "Say the youngsters escape without a hitch and are on their cheerful way to America. *Then* would you consider my offer? If I don't taste you, I'll probably expire of thirst."

"I'll be going with them."

Pursing his lips, he considered this. "I'll meet you in Le Havre. There's a lovely grand hotel—"

"I'm not going to have intercourse with you." She wriggled away from him, doing her best to ignore the curious pulses and aftershocks of what he'd done to her.

"You've said that already," he reminded her with a solicitous smile. "It's a stipulation I've unenthusiastically agreed to."

Veronica attempted to stand on legs now made of wet clay and shot him a look of disbelief. "Then why offer to—that is—what do you get out of it?"

He shrugged. "I've had plenty of orgasms. This was your first. You have some catching up to do. I promise you'll enjoy yourself."

She pressed her hands to fevered cheeks. "The question is why *you* would enjoy it when I'm giving you nothing in return."

"Because..." He lifted his finger and pressed it between his lips, his eyes never leaving hers as he drew it out slowly. "You have no idea how divine you taste."

"Dear God, don't do that." She seized his elbow and tugged on it.

His smile was utterly wicked. "You cannot stop me unless you relent. This cannot be the last time I appreciate flavor of your—"

Surging forward, she slapped a hand over his wicked mouth. "Christ," she huffed.

"Blasphemer." The accusation was muffled by her palm, which he licked, playfully.

Snatching her hand back, she closed her eyes and pinched the bridge of her nose, actively refusing to be charmed. "You're impossible."

"Come now, Countess, you must admit. The danger is splendid, isn't it?"

Her head snapped back up. "What are you talking about?"

"It makes everything better. More intense. The secret meeting in a place we might be discovered. The excitement of a clandestine adventure to facilitate two young lovers. I can see it in your color, in the brightness behind your eyes. You are made for this, and you are magnificent."

"And *you* are categorically mistaken."

He laughed at her then before swooping in for an intoxicating kiss.

"Until tonight, my lady," he vowed before sauntering out and leaving her in the chill of the cargo car, still trembling with the memory of his heat.

And the impossible hunger he'd awakened inside of her.

# Seven

**VERONICA DIDN'T ALLOW** herself to breathe until she spied Penelope Weller and her lover, Adam Grandville, making their careful way toward her on the train platform.

Parisians and travelers blurred together in the colorful chaos of the Gare de Lyon, performing a polite waltz as they either disembarked or boarded the train. Any other day Veronica would have enjoyed the spectacle, but she couldn't allow herself a moment's peace until the train pulled away from the station and the young couple was out of Weller's reach.

Pasting on a smile at their approach, she felt it melt immediately from her face as she took in their identical expressions. "What is it? What's wrong?"

Rather than answer, Penelope and Adam stepped to the side, revealing a third companion.

Adrienne.

She'd a carpet bag gripped in two hands and even the veil of her emerald velvet hat couldn't hide her swollen lip and blackening eye.

*Blast and damn.* While Veronica was dallying with

Sebastian in the cargo car, the poor woman had been suffering her husband's violent displeasure.

"Please don't be cross with us," Adam pleaded earnestly, swiping his fine hat from his dark head to clutch in front of him. "But Penny and I couldn't leave her. I kept thinking...what if she were my own mother? I'd do anything to save her from such a monster."

Veronica had to blink back tears, so touched was she by Adam's decency. A kind heart was often hard to find. Gentlemen abounded these days, but a truly gentle man?

A rare treasure, indeed.

"Adrienne..." Veronica paused, struggling with the secrets she held. "What if I told you that you might very soon become a widow? Would you still want to go? To give up everything your husband might leave you?"

"My husband has nothing but vices and debtors, my lady," the woman answered with downcast eyes. "His wealth has become sham. I will be left with less than nothing...but if I stay, I will become nothing."

"I'm so sorry," Veronica hugged the fragile woman to her.

"Dear Adam has invited me to live with his family in Boston. They've a summer home somewhere called Montauk, right on the sea." The little spark of hope in Adrienne's voice ignited something inside of Veronica as well.

Struck with anxiety, she pulled away. "Of course, you can have my seat on the coach to Le Havre, but are only two tickets on the ship. Your cabins—"

"We'll manage." Adam said with confidence. "This is a trip I've taken often in my life. I can navigate preparations easily."

Veronica found a new appreciation for the lad. He

might look boyish and a bit innocent, even for his age, but he'd the steady gaze of a capable man.

"What about your travel papers?" she remembered with alarm. "I only have two forged copies for Penny and Adam. Should anyone look at the register...they'll know where to find you. Furthermore, you won't be able to board the ship without them."

"I don't care if I'm found, I won't return." Adrienne's eyes blinked against instant panicked tears. "But...*he* keeps my papers and all money. Somewhere in his cabin. He wouldn't tell me where."

Adam stepped forward. "I will go back and get them."

"No." Veronica put a staying hand on his lean chest. "You won't be allowed near his car, as the porters and ushers don't know you. But I've been Penelope's companion since London and will gain easy access." Taking the bag from Adrienne, she pushed it into Adam's hands and pointed to the coach in which she'd hired three seats to Le Havre. "You two help settle her into the coach and let me search for the papers."

Whirling on her bootheel, she dashed back for the train, weaving in and out among some rather incensed travelers.

Lifting her skirts to ascend the steep, unsteady steps to the train, she grasped the large hand that reached down to lift her up and came face-to-face—or face to chest, rather—with Sebastian Moncrieff.

"You came back." His pleased smile broke over her like the rays of spring sunshine dawning over a late winter's night. "Couldn't wait until Le Havre to collect on my promise?"

His what?

A tongue smoothed over his full lip, reminding her what he intended to do.

*Oh...* No. She couldn't think of that now. Couldn't allow the inconsequential parts of her to awaken when she had such an important task in front of her.

Which was?...

*Papers!* Dear God, how was it a man could be so handsome he made her forget what she was about?

Scowling up at him, she snatched her hand from the warmth of his enveloping grip. "Adrienne Weller took my place in the coach. She's leaving him."

His smile became impossibly brighter, revealing both rows of even, white teeth. "Excellent. I applaud her decision. I've been thinking, I could take my blade to Weller now, and then maybe you and I should find a bed here in Paris. It's a city for lovers, after all."

Veronica blinked up at him in disbelief for a split second before shoving her shock aside. "I hardly have time for this—please move." She made to shoulder past him, unsuccessfully.

"What's happened?" he asked, sobering only slightly.

"Adrienne needs her travel papers and I have to retrieve them before the train takes off again."

Sebastian checked a fine watch hanging from his silk vest. "We hardly have time."

"That is precisely what I just said!"

"So it is. What can I do to assist?"

"You can stay out of my way."

To her utter astonishment, he turned to the side like an opening door, making a sweeping motion for her to pass.

She shot forward, painfully aware that she needed to traverse three cars of crowded hallways...

*Drat.* She should have stayed on the platform and boarded on Weller's car, though a look out the window told her the platform was no less congested than the halls.

"Don't follow me," she snapped to Sebastian over her shoulder. "It's conspicuous. Suspicious, even."

"But it isn't," he corrected. "I'm often seen following pretty women."

For some reason, his words tasted both sweet and sour. "You should keep your eye on Weller," she muttered. "That is how you can help."

"I was, but he is busy doing what I'd rather be doing with you."

She turned with an aggravated growl that only seemed to amuse him further. "Might you not be—whatever this is?" She hadn't the words for it.

Charming? No, too infuriating for that.

Romantic? No, too wicked for that.

"I beg you to be silent so that I might focus on the task at hand."

To her surprise, he said not another word, but remained her shadow. It occurred to Veronica to be incensed at his audacity, but then his presence was actually useful. The crowd parted for him like a biblical hero—or plague—making way for the width of his shoulders and the force of his presence. Sebastian Moncrieff didn't merely occupy space. He claimed it. He owned it. He was the master of whatever ground he walked upon, and she was currently under his protection.

A part of her wanted to resent that fact.

To begrudge the feminine pleasure it brought her.

But there wasn't the time for that, either.

When they reached the Weller car, she went straight to Arthur's cabin and began to rifle through the few drawers bolted to the wall by the expensively appointed bed.

In contrast, Sebastian flipped over the mattress and checked within every pillowcase before lifting Weller's entire trunk and dumping the contents on the bed.

That was one way to do it, Veronica supposed.

Finding nothing, she pulled open a cupboard and froze.

"Blast and damn it all! The papers must be in this safe." Stronger curses perched on her lips, but she didn't allow them to escape.

"Say it." The dark command rumbled so close to her ear, she could feel the warmth of his breath tease at wisps of her hair.

"Say what?"

"The word that's itching your tongue. Say it. I imagine it's something like... *Fucking hell.*"

That word.

In her ear.

From behind.

*Fucking.*

"I don't say such things," she informed him, her voice stiffer than her melting legs. "I'm a lady."

"It'll make you feel better," he promised.

Needing him to back away before his scent overwhelmed her, she elbowed him in the chest. Not hard, but enough to feel like she might have elbowed a statue made of granite or marble. "What would make me *feel better* is getting into that safe."

"I could do it, rather easily," he boasted.

She turned around, finding his mouth entirely too close for comfort. "I-I don't believe it."

"Please, this thing is child's play." He lifted one sardonic brow, before drawing his finger down the ridge of her nose as if she were an adorable child. "You *can't* have forgotten I'm a pirate."

She slapped his hand away archly. "Then do it."

"First you have to say it."

"No."

"All right," he almost sang the words while making a dramatic show of checking his watch once more. "I think we've only ten more minutes until we pull away from here. I suppose I should leave you to your—"

She seized his elbow. "Are you really going to abandon—"

He turned back with a sinful smirk. "Come on, my lady, say it."

*Fine.* Fine she would say the bloody word! "*Fucking hell* but you're impossible."

His laugh was low and rich and exasperatingly victorious as he crouched in front of the safe to inspect it. Holding his hand back to her without looking up he said. "I need one of your two-pronged hairpins and that hat pin with the golden feather."

Veronica put her hand up to her braided knot held in place by three stick pins and topped by a little fascinator of dark gold skewered through with a single feather pin.

"The quicker the better, Countess," he prodded.

Plucking the pins from her hair, she took the hat from her head and smoothed her crown with anxious motions. His large fingers made astoundingly deft motions with the delicate pins in the lock and the safe was open in less than half a minute.

Veronica reached in to find the papers conveniently tucked into a well-labeled leather file.

Heedless of the mess, they both burst out the door and made for the rear of the car. Just as Veronica would have leapt from the train onto the platform, she was bodily lifted from around the waist and set behind Sebastian in one graceful sweep.

"Unhand me, you oaf, I have to—!"

Sebastian plucked the papers from her grasp. "I'll get it to them faster."

"But—"

"You go up the train four cars and wait for me there," he instructed. "I don't want you here should Weller wander back whilst I'm gone."

"But you don't know where the coaches are."

"Yes, I do, I saw you return from them."

"You don't know which one the Wellers are in." She swiped for the papers, but he held them out of her reach. "There's no time for this argument, Moncrieff. Give them back."

"Have some faith in me, Countess," he prodded. "A little trust."

"*Me*. Trust *you*? That's rich!"

He looked truly wounded for a moment, which made her angrier.

"Go check on Weller," she suggested. "What if he returns before the train pulls away?"

"I left my valet to watch him," he shrugged.

"You what?"

"Brannock. You met him on the Devil's Dirge. Now, I am not commanding you, but I'm beseeching. Go to my car. Just as a precaution."

He was asking. Not ordering. Had a man ever done that before?

He softly caressed her cheek with the back of his knuckles. They were too rough to belong to an earl, abrading her soft skin enough to lift goosepimples all over her body.

And yet, his eyes were so gentle. So sincere.

With a lithe motion of a sailor, he swung down to the platform, skipping the steps altogether. "I shan't let you down, Veronica," he vowed before surging toward the line of coaches at the end of the vast concourse.

Veronica...

She'd corrected him before. And wanted to again, as he shouldered his way through the crowd.

Because her heart did a little extra beat each time he said her name.

# Eight

SEBASTIAN BROKE into a run as the train chugged into motion.

He bounded around travelers and leapt over porters and their carts of attaché cases. Never having been an apt French student, he only recognized the curse words hurled in his direction and summarily ignored them.

If anyone stood in between him and the raven-haired woman on the platform of his car, their fate was a fault all their own.

Veronica stood clinging to the rail, her eyes owlish with fear as her lips moved in encouragement.

Had she no faith? He would get to her. He would not leave her to face the aftermath of this adventure alone.

Besides, he'd a promise to collect on.

He might have leapt onto one of the cars next to him, but he wanted to reach her. To grip the hand she stretched out, and have no one in between him and the lush bed on the other side of the door.

Spurred by that thought, his legs churned faster beneath him, and his heart pounded in his chest, feeding his body the speed and stamina to leap into her arms right as the platform fell away.

She made a soft squeal of shock as he hauled her into his arms, tugged at the latch to the door, and swept her inside. Throwing the lock, he shut out the East Parisian winter, the Wellers, and the anything that might bring her to her senses before he could get his tongue between her thighs.

The locomotive accelerated beneath them, but Sebastian's own engine was already purring and thrumming, anticipating a rhythm of his own.

He could feel it in her, as well. A pulse of expectancy, the gnawing of primitive hunger awakened.

She'd been given a satisfying appetizer...a mere taste of what he could do.

And now she was ravenous for the meal.

Except he was the one with the watering mouth. *He* was the diner and *she* the feast. And now that he'd done a bit of sprinting, he'd worked up an even greater appetite and warmed up his body to perform.

Trying not to dwell on how perfectly she fit in his arms, he lowered his head to claim a kiss, and was stopped by her fingertips against his lips.

"You saw them pull away?" she asked, anxiety overshadowing the excitement dilating her lovely eyes.

"And turn the corner," he said against her fingertips before gently nibbling on them. "There's no way Weller or anyone else would know where they've gone."

She went lax with relief in his arms, her fingers dropping away from his mouth.

Thus liberated, he took her lips in a searing kiss as he carried her to the lavish coverlet of burgundy velvet embroidered with gold. He draped her across the foot of the bed, her skirts a river of golden silk over a sea of the most luxurious wine. The tableau was so appealing Sebastian stood for a moment to take it all in, seriously questioning for the first time how much self-discipline he'd be able to maintain.

Her sumptuous body, constricted by so many buttons and contraptions to conform an unnatural shape, called to his fingers to unravel the fashion she hid behind. She could craft that image for the world, and it was a lovely picture, indeed. But he wanted her unbound and undone. Exposed to his gaze alone, her beauty unfettered and undeniable.

He wanted it with such violent fervor, he forced himself to stand still. To remind himself of her fragility, of her permissions and her desires. Her past and her fears.

The gods, for some benighted reason, had seen fit to grant him this rare taste of Heaven. He didn't bloody deserve it, but by Jove he would fucking drain every drop. Extend every moment so that he might take the memory and lock it away in that shallow vault of truly joyful reminiscences.

Perhaps this hadn't been a celestial gift to him, but an ultimate, inevitable torment. He'd know perfection, only to have tasted what he didn't deserve.

What he couldn't keep.

Her delicate throat worked over a swallow as she lifted herself onto her elbows, apprehension leaking into her gaze. Her hair had loosened from where he'd taken the pin, and he decided to begin there. It was that or drown in the verdant infinity of her eyes.

"This is one of the first times I've seen you look so serious..." she ventured, as he released the rest of her braids to fall from their confines. "Are you reconsidering—"

"Have you ever enjoyed a book with such delight, that you're afraid to open it again because the turn of each delicious page brings you closer to the end?" He could hardly look at her as he said it, because he meant it too keenly to laugh the truth away. He was forever turning sentiment into a jape, because if it was real...

It was terrifying.

"I—I've often been afraid of losing something so much, that I didn't allow myself to reach for it. I denied myself altogether." She reached up for him, gripping the lapels of his jacket and tugging him down. "What fools we both are."

Her lips rose to meet his in a searing, soul-stealing kiss. This one containing the desire she'd long denied and the hunger long unfulfilled.

Soft, questing hands tucked into the shoulders of his jacket and smoothed it down his arms until it landed in a puddle on the floor.

When her fingers went to his collar to tug at the knot there, Sebastian broke the kiss and gently enfolded both her busy hands into his own. "If you touch my skin, I'll be lost," he confessed, pressing her back to the mattress before making a titillating journey down her body to where her knees draped over the edge. "So you lie back, my lady, and let me play."

"What if I'm already lost?" she asked the ceiling as her chest worked over hastening breaths.

"I hope you lose yourself more than once before I'm through..." As he lowered to his knees before the bed, he smoothed his hands up the silk of her stockings, lifting her skirts along the way. Charting a course over shapely calves, he paused to kiss the dimples by her knees and caress the soft places behind them. Eventually reaching her undergarments, he pulled them over her hips, down her legs, and had to free them as they caught on the hooks of her short boots.

Sebastian loved nothing so much as the sight of a

beautiful naked woman...but somehow the idea of her coming while wearing those boots threatened to drive him out of his mind.

He didn't force her legs apart, merely kneaded at the taut muscles there, eliciting a little whimper as she allowed them to splay open. She couldn't see much over the mountain of skirts he'd rucked up to her waist, and it was just as well.

For surely he looked like a man who'd found an oasis in the middle of the Sahara, and perhaps the intensity of his regard might have overcome her.

The sight of a glistening cunny bared by parted thighs was a thing he always enjoyed.

But this.

*This.*

It wasn't the usual enchantment he experienced. Not merely a delicious thrill of discovery, but something far more powerful.

Indescribable.

Veronica was pink and peach and perfect.

He indulged in the sight for so long, she began to tense and squirm with violated modesty. "Moncrieff? Is everything..."

Her question died on a moan as his fingers petted through the soft triangle there, awakening little quivers that twitched and trembled through her entire lithe body.

God she was so responsive. So prone to unrestrained movement erupting, alongside sighs and sounds so primitive and visceral they mesmerized him. Veronica was a self-possessed woman naturally, but she was also honest.

And good. So fucking good. In every imaginable way.

Sebastian generally left good girls alone. He wasn't

one to delight in deflowering the virgin or teaching the uninitiated. He tended to bed women who could contain his wickedness, and demand a few things of their own.

Why was she different?

Someday, when he wasn't about to taste her sweet sex, he'd take the time to figure it out.

Lowering his head, he dragged his lips across her inner thigh, where the skin was thin and alive with nerves. Once she'd seemed to recover from the shock of his attentions there, he drifted to the seam of her leg and her hip, nuzzling the softness there, before moving to the very core of her.

He hovered for a breathless moment, heart pounding in a rough staccato.

Every muscle knotted with craving.

Sebastian was a man always battling the rule of his fathomless desire, lest he become overwhelmed by them. Tonight...he knelt at the altar and pledged his fealty to a hunger that now demanded his surrender.

Closing his eyes, he drew his tongue up the seam of closed lips, parting them with sinful slowness.

Christ she was, in a word, delectable.

Veronica's entire body jerked, but she made no sound. Not until he reached that soft bud at the apex of those folds. He thought he might have to coax it out, to play in the little pleats and ruffles of flesh until it revealed her need.

But she came to him ready. Not just once, but twice in a day.

Perhaps her heart had been too broken to know desire, or to identify it, but her body... *oh,* her delicious body was a conduit for pleasure. She'd been crafted to tempt, to entice, to lure, and to make love.

She'd been wasted on a cruel man, and her real

tragedy was that she'd ever lived a life without someone to worship her. To make her sing this throaty melody he'd coaxed from deep within her as he nibbled and supped at the edges of her folds, tickling her with his breath. Teasing her with playful lips and gentle flicks of his tongue. Pressing vibrating moans of encouragement against her wet flesh.

*So wet.* So sweet. A nectar only rivaled by ambrosia... And even then.

Between her trembling thighs, he felt like a god. And soon, he'd convert her to belief.

Not in the divine, but in *him.*

*I'll worship your body, my lady,* he thought. *But you'll be praying to me before I'm through.*

Apparently, she'd had enough of his teasing, because she slid impatient fingers through his hair. Pausing, she seemed unsure whether to pull him closer or push him away.

Her features contorted into a mask of misery, but the noises she emitted were raw with pleasure.

Taking pity on her, Sebastian splayed her open with his fingers, thoroughly exposing the little peak of her sex. With slow and tender precision, he pressed the flat of his tongue over the pulsating opening of her body, coating it with her slick desire before drawing it up against the quivering bud.

She made a sound that shot straight to his already aching cock. It kicked against the confines of his trousers as she tugged on his hair with just enough strength to cause a delicious sort of pain.

*Fuck.* He might not survive this.

Drawing upon every ounce of—admittedly under-developed—willpower, he let his tongue slide over and around the delicious little hardness amidst all that soft, pliant flesh. Touching it. Flicking away. A languid stroke. A gentle glide.

She shuddered beneath his ministrations. Said things in a language he didn't recognize. Maybe one that never existed.

His hands had to move to her thighs as he dined, using his strength to keep them plied open so he could work. She bucked and trembled, jerked and moaned, as if he were an inquisitor and the lashing was meted out by a weapon more painful than his tongue.

"Moncrieff," she finally sobbed. "I—I can't—Please. *Please*."

He lifted his head to look up over her body, glad and also bemoaning that he'd kept them both clothed.

Her lush ass fell back to the bed and her legs splayed in an exhausted collapse.

"Sebastian," he said, his breath feathering over her core, causing it to visibly throb.

She seemed unable to speak, blinking down at him in obvious, foggy-eyed confusion.

"I want you to say my name when you come," he ordered in a growl he didn't recognize as his own. It was everything he wasn't. Dark. Demanding. Possessive.

She nodded, curling her pelvis forward in a wordless plea for release.

Lifting a finger, he drew wet little circles around the entrance to her body, probing the tight flesh there until she made a plaintive little sound.

"Say it," he commanded.

"S-Sebastian." Her broken whisper filled him with an emotion he couldn't begin to identify. Something he knew he'd been seeking but didn't know what to do with now.

True to his word, he parted his lips over the little

pearl of her pleasure and insinuated his finger deep into the recesses of her core.

*Fuck.*

*Fuck!* He wished he hadn't done that.

Even as her hips surged up with a sob of bliss, he accepted that he was a fucking doomed man. He'd forever regret knowing what she felt like from the inside. What hot depths of slick velvet pulled at him with such exquisitely feminine flesh.

Everything that had ever happened before, everything that might come to pass after this, dissolved beneath the devastating perfection of the moment. He suckled and slid, licked and laved, all the while rocking his finger inside of her, letting her body drench him with the gripping, pulsating release that took her much too soon.

Thighs clamped against his shoulders and her hands fell to the bed beneath her, bunching and ripping at the coverlet. She screamed in breaths and sobbed his name —or at least raw, broken syllables of it. Over and again. Both an invocation and a benediction, a plea for mercy and a hymn of praise.

Beautiful spasms clenched his fingers, inviting him deeper as she bowed and writhed like a wild creature set free after so long in captivity.

A devil's whisper slithered through him in the dark. *Seduce her. Claim her. Release your cock and finish making her your own.*

*She will not stop you.*

# Nine

**SURGING AWAY FROM HER,** Sebastian stumbled to the small water closet and stuffed himself inside, slamming the door.

Panting as if he'd only just run for the train, he braced both of his hands on the tiny sink and stared at someone he didn't recognize in the mirror.

He'd the same sand-colored hair, once kept long but now cut fashionably tame. The same pale whisky eyes and sunbaked skin, weathered over his brawny bones just enough to leave winsome grooves that deepened when he smiled.

Except now, they were carved with something he'd never spied on his own features. Something he did not battle often. If ever.

Fear.

Stark and sinister, it glared back at him, creating an ugly portrait of features so often and so frankly admired.

In his entire life, he'd given over to indulgence. To a rebellious rejection of all things considered decent. Tasting the vitality of life had become a tonic to the rigid rejections he'd experienced in his youth.

81

And yet, he'd always known what he was doing. What his actions might do to him. He took risks, knowing the outcome always tended to turn in the favor of people like him. Strong. Handsome. Proud. Teutonic. Charming. Male. Skilled. Noble. Educated. Wealthy.

Ruthless.

Indeed, he generally only need smile in the direction of a lady to entice her, and it took a few inviting compliments to see her legs parted.

He couldn't remember the last time he'd been denied something—someone—he wanted.

And here he was, wanting someone more than he could ever remember, and apparently her favorite word was *no*.

It should have been enough.

This taste of her. This pleasure he'd promised. He was a libertine and a hedonist and all the things of which she'd accused him.

By choice. The vices and violence, the pleasure and the pain had been measured and controlled by palatable doses. He'd seen so many other men have their sins turned against them. Losing their money to wagers. Their health to sexual disease. Their dignity to drink or the drugging euphoria of other substances.

He'd flirted with all of it and promised himself to none. He was ruled by his passions, not owned by them.

Until now. Until *her*.

Veronica Weatherstoke was a dangerous phenomenon. An obsession he could feel building in his blood, threatening to overtake him completely.

His entire life he'd spent bedding women who could have no claim to him. Not to his body, his money, his time, nor his heart. Neither did he seek to keep them once he'd had them. Not even a mistress. A handful of lovers had been amusing enough to dally with more than once. But even upon that rare occurrence he'd made certain feelings were never involved.

And the moment a woman twitched a possessive eyelash in his direction, he'd disappeared like smoke in the sea mist.

A pirate's life was lucky in that respect.

Lucky... And lonely.

Why did she make his loneliness feel less like freedom and more like a consequence?

A soft knock on the door caused him to flinch, though he should have known it was coming. He'd left her so abruptly, he couldn't even remember if she'd been finished with her orgasm.

"Moncrieff?" came the hesitant call from the other side.

"I'll be a moment longer," he croaked out, turning on the water to wash his hands and splash over his face, hoping to cool the fever there.

What was he going to tell her?

The woman already didn't trust him, for better reasons than he'd admitted to her. If he told her the truth now, she would run from him in terror.

How could he explain that he'd become so overcome by lust he'd almost lost his humanity? That the sight, and scent, and taste of her pleasure had driven his tattered dignity into the dirt... That he found a quickly fraying thread of decency and used it to shut himself in here.

He'd wanted to take her, in every possible way. To steal her. Claim her. Own her. Possess her.

Only her.

*Always* her.

He'd wanted to thrust himself inside of her body, so that the last man who'd had her was not the monster she'd married. A beast Sebastian carried forward from the seed of his Viking ancestors convinced him he could fuck the memory of any man out of her. Could turn her into a vessel for him, alone. To shape her to his cock...

And even *that* wasn't the worst of it.

Images of her, wrapped in the richest fabrics he could provide and adorned in gems he'd draped over her, glittered in his mind's eye. While he'd had his tongue buried in the most wicked parts of her, his imagination had summoned other fantasies.

Ones he'd never before entertained.

If he could make her come, could he make her laugh? Could he make her feel safe and protected?

Could he make her happy?

Make her *his*?

Groaning, he ran his hand over his face, doing his best to wipe away the lunacy.

He was not a man a woman would want to keep.

The knock sounded again, this time more urgent. "Is everything...are you all right?"

Categorically not.

Sebastian looked down to where his cock throbbed painfully against the placket of his trousers. Even the fine fabric felt like sandpaper against the sensitized flesh.

Perhaps if he relieved his pent-up desire, some of the madness would abate. At the very least, he'd be able to think more clearly.

"I'll only be a—" He gasped in relief as he undid his trousers and released the shaft into his hand.

"Sebastian?"

*Yes. Say my name.* The column flexed in his grip, a bead of moisture trickling from the head.

"A moment, Countess, *please*," he implored. I can't—"

The door slid open, and there she stood, silently taking stock of him.

His brain stalled completely at the sight of her. Flushed with passion and her pale skin painted with shadows, she was the purest vision, and he was a vulgar catastrophe.

And yet, Sebastian could do nothing but remain as he was. One hand on the sink, the other around his sex.

God, but even the calluses on his palms was torture.

His gaze lowered to her hands. So soft. Supple.

"I need you to go," he gritted through clenched teeth.

Rather than turn away, she took a step forward, eyes both hot and soft. "I *know* what you need."

Sebastian had always been a man of action, but he found himself transfixed to stillness as she reached for him, first touching his shoulder, her fingers warm and tentative through the thin shirt. Both of their eyes followed her questing hand as she stroked down the curve of his bicep, to his elbow, and traced the veins in his forearm down to his wrist.

They both caught their breaths as her cool fingers joined his. Her touch seared through his shaft like a shock of lightning, pulling his balls in tight to his body and causing an involuntary convulsion of pure, electric pleasure.

He released himself to her softer, smoother grip with a helpless, wordless sound.

She joined him in the mirror, her features at once serene and knowing. Benevolent and bold. The most beautiful woman on Earth. And he?

Checking his own reflection, he quickly looked away. Who was this creature he'd become? Wild-eyed and flushed with reckless dread. A sheen of sweat at his hairline. Every muscle tightened over his thick bones in a mask of agonizing bliss.

Just when he thought he could take no more, her head lowered, disappearing from the view of the glass.

Releasing the sink, his body turned to face her as she blocked the door with the pool of her golden skirts as she sank to her knees.

*Holy God.*

Usually, he'd be goading a generous lover on with sinful encouragements, lacing his fingers through her hair and massaging her scalp. Touching her mouth, sinking his fingertips into it.

But he did none of those things as her hand remained gently locked around him, her mouth tantalizingly close.

When her breath caressed the throbbing tip of his sex, his knees weakened.

When she slid soft, curious lips over the thick head, they buckled completely.

He caught himself by slamming his palms into each wall at his side, pressing out like Sampson—hoping these barriers would hold.

Nothing about her ministrations were particularly skilled or confident, and in that he found even more satisfaction. Her lips were full pillows of pleasure, her mouth smooth and hot, slick and succulent. Her tongue, tentative and curious, found thrilling little ridges and sensitive veins beneath the thin skin stretched over steel. Each stroke sent delirious sensations surging through him to dizzying effect.

He searched his empty mind for something to say until her eyes locked with his. The need to speak died as something so tender and profound passed between them, he dared not profane it with words.

After her initial exploration of his sex, her motions became bolder. Her eyes blazed up at him, eternal wells of jade desire, as she took him as deep as possible, then sucked with a gentle brutality as she drew her head back. The many inches she could not take, she stroked with her palm, moistened by her mouth and his need.

Sebastian panted like a wolf after taking down a fresh kill. Blessing her and cursing her as his emotions varied violently from heart-rending tenderness to demanding desperation. Nothing in this world could be so sweet as this goddess on her knees, tending to his cock.

When she used her tongue to swirl around his head in rhythm to her strokes, he caved in upon himself a little, seeking to pull away before the pressure gathering in his spine found its escape into her awaiting mouth.

"Stop," he rasped. "If you don't, I'll—"

She gripped him harder, increased her pace as he grew larger against her lips. The desperate pull of his muscles locking down tore away the last vestiges of his control as his climax gathered in his blood.

He threw his head back with a primal roar as his hips jerked once, twice, and then his entire body was imprisoned by pleasure. Incapacitated by pulsating ropes of velvet and silk.

He belonged to her now.

She'd drained the very substance of his life and swallowed it. Consumed him with warm little licks and soft, encouraging sounds until he was nothing but her leftover scraps.

Happily so.

She could discard him at her will. Throw him to her hounds, and he'd lie there and yearn for her as he was ripped apart. For another touch. For another kiss. Just one more taste.

When he was able, he reached down and hauled her to her feet, crushing both her body and her mouth to his.

This time, she met him with equal fervor, her

tongue sparring brazenly as they melded the flavors of the other into one irresistible sexual delicacy.

Never in his life had Sebastian savored anything so sweet.

By the time she broke the kiss they were both struggling for breath. She tucked her head against his chest as she visibly sought control of her lungs.

Calling upon one final, rational thought, he disengaged his hips to tuck his sex back into his trousers, chagrined to discover he was still half-hard. After such a powerful release, he'd expect to need at least half an hour to fully recover.

As it was now, he wasn't certain he ever would.

"You didn't have to do that," he said, concerned by the tension in her body against his.

"I needed to," she said, her forehead still pressed into his clavicles as if she couldn't extricate herself to face the enormity of what they'd done. "I-I wanted to."

Swamped with compassion, he smoothed unsteady hands over her shoulders. "Tell me what you are thinking," he murmured, pressing a kiss into the wreck he'd made of her tidy hair.

She still didn't look up, so he had to strain to hear her. "Would it be possible to—I know this isn't what— that we aren't—but... I..." Several unformed sentences died with a trembling sigh.

Hooking a finger under chin, he pulled away so he could lift her gaze to his. "Tell me what you need."

She pressed her lips together, gathering strength. "Would you...hold me?"

"Woman, if you asked me to, I'd hold up this train."

He turned her around and did his best not to stumble as he directed her toward the bed. It was difficult not to sweep her up and carry her, but something stopped him. Not just the lack of available space in a railcar, but also a sense that she needed her physical autonomy just now.

Taking the initiative, he sat on the bed and reached for her, allowing her to slide between his open legs and once again tug at the silk knot at his throat.

"I know I'm ridiculous," she said with a self-effacing smile. "But I can't relax knowing this is tight and confining."

"Undress me at your leisure, my lady," he teased, hiding a spill of bittersweet warmth in the cavern of his ribs.

"I *won't* be undressing you," she informed him crisply. "I just need you to be comfortable."

That warmth... It spread like sun-warmed honey through his limbs as he sat with uncharacteristic stillness, submitting to her ministrations.

Her eyebrows drew together as she plucked and grappled at the loops he'd secured rather tightly.

*I need you to be comfortable.*

How many women had told him they needed him? Too many to remember.

In fact, he'd forgotten every single one... Every woman who'd ever needed him. To fuck them. To adore them. To pleasure, arouse, and excite them.

Women were often very generous, especially in bed. It was one of the things Sebastian loved about them the most.

But never in his life had one offered something so genuine and uncomplicated as this. A consideration of his simple comforts.

Sebastian could not detect one hint of sex or seduction in her movements, no coy glances from beneath her lashes. No moistening of lips. Just concentration, and eventually, victory, as she finally grappled it loose and slid the offending tie from his neck.

He swallowed, unencumbered by the garment, and still something threatened to choke him with a suspicious heaviness in his throat. Something concerning.

Terrifying, even.

Women had undressed him before. Had stayed for a cuddle, a drink, or even a night.

But never in his life had he felt such intimacy. Such immense vulnerability. This was no prelude to wickedness, but a quiet aftermath.

Something a wife would do.

Unstitched by the thought, he reached for her, smoothing his hands over the shape of her slim waist confined in her corset. "Should I unlace you?"

She shook her head, parting only a few buttons of his collar and splaying it open before she nudged him to lie down.

Sebastian did as she directed, stretching long across the bed and creating a cradle for her head in the divot between his shoulder and chest. She settled in exactly the place he'd hoped, fitting against him like a missing piece of a puzzle before resting a hand on his breastbone.

How strange to be so tranquil and unnerved at the same time, he thought as his arms encircled her.

They lay there for a silent moment, their muscles melting together, breaths slowing and eventually synchronizing as Sebastian watched the play of the lantern light on the canopy above.

Never in his life had he sat in silence with a woman, not contentedly at least.

What was Veronica Weatherstoke doing to him? What sort of man would she make of him if they spent more than these precious hours in each other's company?

It was a question he couldn't allow himself to ponder. So, he posited one to her instead, one he'd been contemplating since rediscovering her on this train.

"What keeps you from allowing me to make love to you?" He kept his tone casual, as if the answer meant nothing more to him than any passing curiosity. "Are you afraid I'll get you pregnant?"

Her head shook against his arm. "It isn't that... In fact, I don't think you could."

He grunted. "I assure you, Countess, I come from a *very* fertile line of—" He felt tension steal back into the hand at his chest, bunching her shoulders closer to her neck.

*Not everything is about you.* He chided himself, feeling like an absolute ass. "You mean you are not able to..."

"I don't think I am," she said matter-of-factly, though the tension didn't abate as she idly plucked at a button on his shirt. "Surely you don't want to talk about sad things just now."

His hand stroked up the soft arm of her gown, and he lifted it to her hair to finish unraveling the few onyx braids that remained intact. "I find I want to know all your secret joys and sorrows."

She nuzzled in deeper, allowing him more access to her hair. "More sorrow, I'm afraid," she admitted without dramatics. "Though I'm learning to find joy. To...allow myself the opportunities for discovery and the liberties of pleasure."

"I suppose children are not conducive to liberty," he postulated.

"Though I know they can become great sources of joy." A long breath left her deflated against him as he finished with her braids. Meticulously, Sebastian combed thick fingers through the silken waves of her hair, sifting through little knots or tangles with infinite care, and then massaging the scalp. It was something he'd enjoyed when his locks had been long, and he sought to give her the same shivering delight.

"I am sorry that you were ever denied joy..." he whispered.

A kiss tickled his rib through the thin cotton of his shirt. "I conceived once," she confessed after another silent beat. "Early on in my marriage. But in my third month, Mortimer...he...he kicked me in the stomach, and I lost the child."

A red-hot rage poured through Sebastian's entire being, setting his cursed soul on fire. He took out the memory of Mortimer Weatherstoke's death and relived it with effusive, savage delight.

Thank God the bastard had never been able to procreate.

The dark, selfish thought was accompanied by shame.

Sebastian himself was proof one didn't turn out like one's father. And perhaps a child would have made her life less frightening and lonely. Or conceivably she'd have been subjugated to the hell of a mother forced to watch her husband hurt their child.

The very idea tore through him with claws and teeth, shredding the sweet languor he'd enjoyed only moments before. He shouldn't have asked the question, not only for his own benefit, but he was certain she'd rather not relive the agony.

Veronica smoothed patient hands over his shoulder. "I don't want your fury," she said, low and gentle. "It is done. He is gone from this world, from my life, thanks in part to you."

"I only regret it was not my hand that wielded the blade." He didn't realize he'd spoken the wrathful wish until she replied.

"The Rook had more reason. I'm glad he took his vengeance."

Sebastian didn't argue the point, Mortimer had kept Ash and Lorelai from each other for almost twenty years. He was the reason the boy had become the Rook...had survived the pits of Hell to bring his damned soul back to the woman he'd loved as a child. To inflict his wrath on the foul fiend who'd separated them for no reason but his own cruelty.

But Mortimer Weatherstoke spent a handful of years *hurting* the woman that Sebastian was—

Was what?

He couldn't even think the words... Could not turn the strange maelstrom of his emotion into a tangible thing.

He didn't know how.

What he did know was that she'd asked him to stow his anger. She needed his deference. His gentility. His understanding. He could grant her those things and indulge in his own rage later.

It was the least he could do.

"You don't have to tell me anything," he said, measuring his voice. "But it might do you some good to unburden your mind."

She took in a preparatory breath. "I never conceived after that. Some doctors said my womb was too small, others that my body temperature was too low, or things weren't...shaped correctly inside of me. I was examined in all manner of ways, and no one could give me an answer."

That did less than nothing to abate his ire. "What about your husband? Was he examined?"

The question seemed to startle her. "No one...no one suggested that the fault might lie with him."

"Unbelievable," he snapped. "There's every chance the infertility is his."

93

"Oh? Are you a doctor as well as a pirate and an earl?" she asked, with surprising levity.

"Obviously not. But surely if a woman can...malfunction internally, it stands to reason that a man would as well. There's no way to look inside of our bodies, so who is to say what...pipes and channels and bits and bobs could be defective. It only stands to reason."

"I love that you think that, but the medical community seems to agree that if a man can finish then he is able to breed."

He snorted his naked derision. "I think they'll someday figure out that I was right, and then I'll delight in telling you that I had once informed you thusly."

She let out a soft little sound of mirth. "I look forward to you finding me on that day."

Finding her? Where would she be?

Then it dawned on him, stealing his breath with the bloody obviousness of it all.

Of course, they would go their separate ways. Would she even want to see him again after this?

Was tonight all they had?

There was a man he needed to murder several railcars away. A room they'd ransacked that would be discovered before morning. Questions regarding a missing family that would most certainly arise once the patriarch was found dead.

Pure unmitigated chaos would ensue.

Would she disembark the train now that Penelope and her intended had escaped? And even if Veronica remained until Constantinople, they'd run out of track eventually. What then? Back to her life at Southbourne? Paris? London?

Swallowing a surge of unexpected misery, he allowed

himself to ask another question burning within him for the past year.

"Do you see them often, Lorelai and Ash?"

"All the time. She is my closest friend and I find I like Ash the more I am in his company."

"And..." He drew little circles around her knuckles with an errant finger. "They fare well?"

"They are disgustingly happy."

He was glad to hear it. Truly.

"Why are you not with them? It will be Christmas soon."

She shifted as if the question had made her uncomfortable. "They're newlyweds, and I wanted them to adjust to life together without me being a dark cloud over their happiness. Reminding them of just how it had fallen apart in the first place."

"Lorelai fought for you. She adores you. And the Rook—Ash—is used to having people to care for. He wouldn't mind you sheltering under his roof, beneath his wing. I know him well."

"I believe you, but I left for selfish reasons, as well. When two people are so entwined, being an outsider is almost cruel, and I wanted some space from Southbourne. I'd been a prisoner there for so long, I'd seen very little of the world. I wanted to travel, design and make my dresses, and fall in love with other places in the world. To see women of beauty in every shape, color, and culture. To find textiles made in foreign and exciting places. To find other passions..."

"Other men?"

She scoffed. "I have very little use for other men. The last thing I considered is confining myself to another husband. I have enough money to live on the rest of my life, if I'm frugal, and my creations are lovely supplements to my income."

"How very independent of you."

Lifting herself onto her elbow, she frowned down at him. "Don't be cruel."

"I mean it." He reached up to sift fingers through the silken waterfall he'd made of her hair. "I admire your ambition. I do not blame you for wanting to remain free. I have always lived just so and realize now more than ever what a privilege that is. It is why I joined up with the Rook in the first place. Why that part of my life was so important to me."

His answer seemed to mollify her, but then she blinked down at him with naked speculation.

"Then why did you betray him?"

## *Ten*

**VERONICA BECAME SUDDENLY** afraid that the truth would drive her from his arms.

She didn't want that. Not yet.

What kept her pressed against him was the certainty she felt that he would tell her the truth. She was coming to learn that Sebastian Moncrieff was many things, but not a liar.

Even if that honesty was cruel, as truth often tended to be.

In the pregnant silence that followed her question, she took the moment to truly appreciate the sumptuous railcar splashed in the golden glow of lamplight. The sway of the train beneath them had lulled her into a gentle torpor cocooned in immense masculine heat. Somehow, it'd made her feel safe enough to speak about the past and the pain she'd left in it. And for once in her adult life, she'd allowed herself to trust the sense of security she'd found in his embrace.

It was beyond reason, really, when he'd been such a villainous figure in the lives of those she called family. Ash had been so angry at Sebastian, it'd taken an act of God to keep them from spilling each other's blood.

But Veronica had learned that villains were often the protagonists of their own narratives.

She remained silent as she watched a plethora of emotion darken his resplendence, and gave him the time he needed to truly contemplate her question.

She'd been married to a villain, and though she'd considered Sebastian a diabolical, even deviant degenerate, the word "villain" never truly stuck.

Even when she was the one to hurl it at him.

It was why she'd been able to do what she'd done for him, even after vowing that life would never again find her on her knees for another man.

He didn't ask her to. Didn't push her head down toward his lap, nor did he make her feel guilty for her pleasure when she offered him none in return.

Sebastian Moncrieff had kept his word and respected her wishes... He'd asked nothing of her and delivered what he'd promised.

Of course, he was a beautiful specimen of a man, but that fact was what had made him truly irresistible to her.

Her entire life she'd been expected to exist at the whims and for the pleasure of men. How easy it had been to offer *him* pleasure, when he'd not demanded it from her. How delightful she'd found his astonished reaction.

When she'd found the act otherwise demeaning, she found power on her knees. She'd known, somehow, that he was her creature. Her beast.

Her villain.

Finally, after the silence stretched into a tangled, uncomfortable place, the man beneath her tilted his chin away and studied the canopy while a long exhale deflated him.

"You don't have to tell me," she recanted, searching for a way back to their intimacy of before.

"It's a question I often ponder," he responded, his fingers still tangled in her hair, though he couldn't seem to meet her gaze. "And all the answers that present themselves feel inadequate and pathetic."

She knew he'd done wrong by his friend, and by hers, but the despondency in his voice tugged at a deep-seated sympathy in her soul.

"If I've learned anything in life, it's that anger is little more than fear, pain, or grief wearing a protective mask." She fidgeted with the finely stitched hem of his collar. "You were so furious at Ash," she recalled. "Was it because he'd hurt you, he'd taken something from you, or he'd made you afraid?"

"Do I have to pick only one?" he scoffed.

"Of course not." She waited patiently for him to gather a few more thoughts, discovering the soft golden hairs fleecing his breastbone with curious fingertips.

"You asked me once how I'd escaped a prison sentence," he said stonily, his dazzling eyes dulled as they remained locked on the canopy above them.

"You're changing the subject," she gently chided.

"Not really."

"What do you mean?"

He hazarded a glance at her, and what she read in it broke her heart. She'd expected defiance and excuses and his singular sense of blistering humor.

What she found was a bleak, fathomless indignity.

His gaze skittered away when he spoke again, as if he couldn't both look at her and examine himself at the same time.

"I'm not the Earl of Crosthwaite," he confessed to the shadows above. "My mother, may she rest in peace, was trapped in a loveless marriage to an impotent earl. She had a lover, several in fact. None of them noble."

"Do you know which one of them sired you?" she queried.

"I don't even think she did, or she died before she was able to reveal it to me or the earl."

"And the earl always understood you were not his progeny, for obvious reasons..."

Sebastian shifted, and when she would have raised herself to give him more room, his arms tightened around her, keeping her close. "He hated me for it, but he hated worse the cousin that would inherit. Though, to save face, he named me his heir, and publicly claimed me as his own. Privately, I lived my youth as a prisoner of his rage."

"That's awful," Veronica murmured, pressing a hand to his chest.

"It wasn't so bad. The earl trotted me out when he was supposed to. Granted me the education due my station—er—his station. All the while, he pissed away any inheritance, ruined my childhood home, and dismantled all other properties that might have provided income. I swear to Christ, he even salted the earth in the fields. And so, when he died, I was seventeen and left with nothing but tax debt and a title I'd usurped through no fault of my own. I was the Earl of Nothing."

"That must have been so lonely," she commiserated, resting her chin on the meat of his chest.

He summoned a wan smile that must have meant to be cheerful, but fell short of the mark. "I've never wanted for company," he boasted, more out of habit than pride, she thought.

"Yes, but don't you find that sometimes a crowded room is the loneliest place in the world?"

He tucked her hair behind her ear, stroking at the little diamond bob in her lobe. "Stop looking into my soul, Countess, especially when I'm trying to bare it to you. Sometimes it feels you know me better than I know myself."

Driven by a quick impulse, she pressed a soft kiss to his cheek. "So, you took to the sea to find your fortune," she prompted.

He gave her an arrested stare before continuing. "Fortune found me on the Devil's Dirge, where I climbed in rank rather quickly as I proved my usefulness to the Rook. Eventually we formed a kinship. The Rook violently obtained things, and I violently enjoyed those things.

For me, pirating had begun as a rush of life-affirming exhilaration. The freedom of calling no man king and no country home. And then, it was about something bigger than myself, as well. Revenge on the very system that still took liberty from others. The seas are such a dangerous and wild place...not only because of nature, but because of the types of men that move goods around the world. It was the Rook's own tragic story that tied me to him so utterly."

"Which brings us to the betrayal in question," he said, seeming to notice the confusion wrinkling her forehead. "What the Rook didn't know—what I'd never told him—was that he'd become a brother to me. We'd planned to follow that ancient Roman treasure, the Claudius Cache, to the end of the world, and then retire to paradise. We'd even spoken of doing exactly what I do now, finding the bastards who make a living off the broken backs of shanghaied men, and helping them from this world, starting with your late husband."

Suddenly it all made sense to Veronica...and she finished the story, herself. "But instead, he found Lorelai—and me—and in doing so, he connected with his past and the brothers he'd left there, neither of whom were fond of you or his life as a pirate."

His jaw hardened as he dipped it in verification of her assessment. "I knew the life he was thinking of building with Lorelai, Blackwell, and Cutter had no room for me or the rest of the crew of the Devil's Dirge in it. The future we'd been working toward was quickly disappearing and...and I did something drastic to—I don't know—to snap him out of it all, I suppose. But Lorelai was never truly in danger, I simply figured If I took her with me to find the Claudius Cache, he'd see her next to it and realize what treasure truly was."

"Which he did," she said gently. "Just not in the way you intended."

"I never understood the decision he made..." He lifted his hands until they both cupped her jaw with infinite tenderness, his eyes bright and fervid as he gazed up at her.

"Until now."

## Eleven

**THE KISS WAS** one of equal fervency and mutual need.

Veronica couldn't say which of them had made the first move or the response to it. Their mouths simply met.

Melded.

And the rest of them seemed to follow. Their torsos, hips, legs...

Hearts.

The man beneath her was no longer a creature of charm and mirth or of mischief and wickedness. He was real. A man with arcane depths and the capability for profound compassion.

He'd bared that part of himself to her, which had somehow made her want to see more.

To see everything.

As they devoured each other, her fingers found the buttons of his shirt, and began to tug restlessly, freeing them one by one.

His hands buried themselves in her hair as a guttural groan urged her on.

Finally, she laid the shirt open, displaying an impeccably sculpted torso dusted with hair only slightly darker than his mane. Her fingers slid over taut skin, jolted by an almost electric sensation that coursed through her entire body, landing heavy and hard in her core.

Pulling back, she broke the kiss, momentarily entranced by the glisten on his swollen lips as he watched her with rapt eyes. Motionless. Vigilant. As if she were a bunny that might bolt into the underbrush at the first sign of danger.

Emboldened, Veronica smoothed both hands over his wide shoulders and meandered down the mounds of muscle on his chest and lower, discovering the spectacular corrugations of his torso.

The tendons of his neck tensed and flexed, his jaw clenching and grinding against a powerful need.

Pausing, Veronica glanced down to the bulge straining against his trousers.

*Never again.* She'd once vowed. Never would she lie beneath a man and let him rut and sweat and dump his seed inside her. Never would she be made to feel like some rubbish receptacle after, lying used and discarded on the bed in a puddle of her own tears and shame.

And yet, today seemed like a day for breaking those vows. She'd also promised never to be on her knees before a man, and she'd enjoyed every moment she'd had him in her mouth. His scent, his taste, his heat and girth and shape. The circumference of him matched his own impressive dimensions, and still she was not afraid.

She was not afraid...

A myriad of emotion swirled within her. Arousal, excitement, curiosity, hope...

But not a single hint of fear.

She'd tasted the ocean on his lips when he'd kissed her after. And he'd tasted his own release as well, lingering on her tongue. Their release had created a heady mélange of flavors and erotic delicacy that undoubtedly belonged together.

Her body fit so perfectly next to his, soft and round where his planes were hard and unyielding.

So far, he'd surpassed every previous interaction she'd had with her husband, the only other man with whom she'd been intimate.

Could he pleasure her from the inside as well?

"I want you," she whispered, her body suddenly thrumming with the truth of those words.

He levered up to sit, the motion doing intriguing things to his abdominals as she melted away from his chest to kneel across from him. "What are you saying?" He eyed her warily.

"I want you, Sebastian Moncrieff," she told him, her voice stronger this time. "I want you to take me like that woman on the desk."

He reached out to caress her face. "Not like that, Veronica, not you. I will be gentle and—"

"No." She reached for the lapels of his shirt, yanking them down the cords of his impressive arms as a violent maelstrom gathered within her. "You've shown me gentle. You've given me that. But I don't feel gentle anymore. I want you to take me like you took the women whose stories made you one of the most infamous lotharios in the Empire." Climbing into his lap, she straddled him. "I can't explain this... the violence of this hunger, but it has eaten at me since the day I watched you with that woman and hated her for having what I wanted. What I was *afraid* to want."

She bracketed his face with both her hands, gazing deep into Brandywine eyes, alight with a fire she now understood. "I don't want to be afraid anymore. I want to meet you as an equal, do you understand? I want to feel the full force of your desire, whatever that is."

His nostrils flared as he sat beneath her, every muscle rigid as even the air seemed to still around them. "You have to be *sure*."

She kissed him. Hard and fast. "I'm sure."

A demonic smile toyed with the edge of his lips, as the banked coals in his gaze became a pagan inferno. "So be it."

Without warning, he reached up and rent her bodice down the middle, sending little pearl buttons scattering to the whims of fate, their clatter eaten up by the sounds of the train. In several rather deft and mystifying motions, he'd stripped away the torn fabric, corset, and chemise, and tossed them into the shadows.

Before they landed, she was suddenly on her back beneath him, looking up in limp, open-mouthed astonishment as he divested her of her skirts and undergarments, peeling them from her body with unholy expertise.

Veronica didn't know whether to be impressed or jealous as he discarded it all to the foot of the bed. And then, she forgot what she'd been thinking about when his trousers and boots disappeared.

He was on her before she could recover, a low growl reverberating through his throat as he looked at her as if he'd unwrapped the only gift he'd ever desired.

A hand closed over her breast, his palm abrading the sensitive peak budded from the winter chill and the ferocity of her arousal. He stroked and caressed her, molding her like clay in a sculptor's hand, as his lips found the protuberant nipple and teased it into an almost painful peak.

She'd already been wet for him, ready, but now she released a river of need, her loins melting and pooling in preparation for him. With a throaty sound she didn't recognize as her own, she arched into his mouth, fingers digging into his scalp.

After ravishing one breast, and then the other, he dragged his mouth down a few of her ribs, angling for her sex.

"No." She tugged at his hair to stop him, and he looked up over her body with a wordless question. "Just... Just... Be with me?" Her cheeks burned as she manifested what she wanted into words. Words that now seemed almost inadequate for what she asked of him.

He kissed the thin, sensitive skin beneath her breast with a mischievous smile. In one, smooth, graceful, ever so predatory motion, he moved up her body, lifting her knee to wrap around his hip.

His thick sex slid into the folds protecting the tender opening to her body. "I am with you, Countess."

"Then...please."

"Please, what?" he gritted, as he paused above her to search her face. The muscles in his neck seemed tight enough to tear, and the brackets around his neck were now deep grooves of restraint.

The bastard was going to make her say it. "Fuck me."

With an animalistic sound, he buried his face in the curtain of hair next to her ear, and buried his cock deep in her body.

A strangled gasp of surprise wrenched from her, as little jolts of discomfort accompanied the pleasure.

He hovered for a moment above her, his arm bunching with strength as he supported his weight, the other gripping her thigh, as she wrapped it tighter against his waist.

"Sweet fuck, you're wet. Warm. Tight. Perfect.

*God*." Each word escaped on a breath as he remained still, allowing her to adjust to his intrusion.

How had she never known it was supposed to be like this? No sting or struggle. No pain or bearing down against the clench of her body. She was so struck by the disparity between this moment and the act she'd suffered with her husband, tears burned behind her eyes.

Happy ones.

This was what it was like to welcome a man into her body.

Veronica luxuriated in the fullness. The tensile heat of him above her, inside of her. Hard and smooth and hot everywhere. A feverish beast of flesh and steel.

A sudden, primal need to move overtook her, and she opened wider beneath him, lifting her hips in an invitation to move.

Sebastian choked on a groan, but he obeyed her silent command, rocking his hips at first, testing her reactions with motions both careful and sure. Her name tore from his throat, raw and untuned, lost to the sounds of the storm gathering around them both.

She clung to him, lifting her other leg to take him deeper, hooking her calves around the curve of his muscular ass.

Sebastian didn't kiss her. He didn't croon sweet nothings or smooth at her hair.

He watched.

Every twitch of her muscles, every flutter of her lashes. When she parted her lips, and how fast her breath sawed in and out of her as he moved. Modulating his rhythm to her silent instructions, he went deeper, harder, faster until she was a wild, inarticulate thing only made of chaos and bliss. Her nails bit into his arms and raked down his back, her teeth bared at him more than once until he finally snarled back his reply, slamming his hips against hers in a merciless war for release.

Her ascension was like the train beneath them. Rhythmic, unstoppable, storming through her with all the speed man could muster, and letting every vessel and sinew, top to toe, aware of its ephemeral presence.

Dimly, she heard a guttural roar above her. Felt him clench and tremble as his motions became less measured and more frenzied.

Then they were clenched in a freefall like eagles, the ground rushing toward them.

Let it. She didn't care. She could be dashed on the rocks and not feel a thing but the molten pleasure of her blood and bliss of his hot seed spilling against her womb.

Veronica was nothing but a limp puddle of exhaustion when his forehead finally came to rest against hers. They breathed together in the silence for a moment. Eyes open. Bodies joined.

After a tender kiss buttoned closed the wildness of their joining, he lifted himself away from her and went into the washroom. Returning with a cloth, he washed her, saying soft things she couldn't understand, let alone reply to.

He left again and returned without the cloth to extinguish the lights and slide them both beneath the sheets. Arranging the covers around her, he made a nest with the curve of his body and pulled her into it.

Nestling in, Veronica realized she'd barely slept since London. Due to anxiety over the Wellers and the success of this plot...

Fear and uncertainty hovered in the cold outside of their cocoon. There was so much still unsaid between them.

"Don't do that," he breathed against the crest of her ear, nibbling at it without teeth.

"Hmmm?" She still couldn't summon the strength to form actual syllables.

"Don't start dreading tomorrow. The light will dawn, my lady, and all will be well. We will say the things we cannot say in the dark."

That's what he didn't understand, she thought as she wriggled closer to his big body, allowing the hairs on the tops of his thighs to tickle her backside.

She could tell him anything in the dark. That she was becoming attached to him. That she'd been thinking of him. Mourning him. Missing him. Fantasizing about him. These were little secrets she could share under the cover of night.

But the light of day was for truths. And the truth was that Sebastian Moncrieff might think of her fondly as a one-time lover...

Veronica, however, would never stop yearning for the safety of his arms.

For this.

She would never stop wanting him, even as he walked away.

# Twelve

VERONICA HAD awoken wrapped in Sebastian's dark scent and the luxurious memory of their lovemaking. Momentarily, she'd forgotten that the world was waiting to tear them apart, until she reached over and found his side of the bed empty.

Now she raced as fast as a body was able down the dark, cramped hallways of the train, praying she wasn't too late.

They were pulling away from Venice in the wee hours of the morning. A scant few passengers were up and about. They peered at her as if trying to figure out if she were a ghost or a madwoman as she ran, barefoot and clad in naught but her chemise and a belted velvet smoking jacket she'd found in his wardrobe.

What if it was already too late? What if she couldn't change his mind? What if—

An arm snaked around her waist from behind, and she was hauled into a cabin with two benches facing the other. Only a stunned squeak escaped before a large hand clamped over her mouth.

"What the hell are you doing?" demanded a familiar voice from behind her.

*Sebastian. Thank God.*

She wriggled and writhed until he loosened his hold and took his hand from her mouth. "I came to find you."

"Dammit, Veronica, I could have been in the middle of—"

She seized his lapels. "Tell me Weller is still alive."

"Why?" He eyed her skeptically. "There's no decent reason to wish him so."

"I realized something when I woke and you were not there," she panted, noting an indefinable flare in his eyes as she struggled to regain her breath. "You've been going about this all wrong."

His gaze became as flat as his tone as he replied, "Is that so?"

"Weller may be higher up in this Shanghai operation, but he's not the head. Perhaps the neck, or even the hands—it doesn't matter." She waved the metaphor away. "What is important is the information he could give you. If your design is to dismantle the entire system, you'll need names, places of contact, ports of refuge for these criminals. You are an earl with a seat in this empire and a voice that demands to be heard. Not only are you wealthier than most men can imagine, but you are a born leader." She shaped her hands to his jaw and stared hard into his eyes, willing him to mark her. "You have power, Sebastian, *use* it. Use it to do good. To be better."

He covered her hands with his, pulling them away from his face and encompassing his fingers in her own. "I told you, I'm not a good man. I'm wicked and—"

"I know!" She jerked her hands from his grasp. "But you can be wicked and still do the right thing sometimes. Yes?"

To her amazement, he laughed. Low and rich with a mercurial glimmer in his dazzling eyes.

"I fail to see what is so funny," she said testily, trying not to lose her hope.

"I can't lie to you, my lady." He reached for her hand again and brought it to his lips to press a reverent kiss on the knuckles. "The authorities are holding Weller in Venice until Scotland Yard can send someone to oversee the extradition. He will be tried for his crimes... and interrogated as to his associates."

Stunned, she stared at him as the lights of the Italian coast played havoc with his skin and bounced off the fair streaks in his untidy hair. They'd not spoken of this. Last she knew his plan was to murder the man. "Why—why did you do that?"

"Because I knew you'd want me to." Sliding his thumb into her clenched fist, he pried her fingers open and dragged his lips against her open palm.

"Ohhhhh..." She hadn't meant to moan that.

"And..." He drew the word out between playful samples of the delicate skin on the underside of her wrist. "Because it was the right thing to do."

"The—the right thing?"

He released her hand and took a step back, holding her only with a solemn gaze that sat stark and strange on a face as splendid as his. "I realized something as well, Countess, when I woke to find you beside me."

Lanced by anxiety, she hitched in a preparatory breath. "Oh?"

"I know you never want to feel beholden to another man, and that is your prerogative. But I am yours, Veronica Weatherstoke. Body, heart, and soul. I give myself to you freely and without reservation, to do with whatever you wish."

Her heart sputtered, stalled, and then kicked over in her ribs twice as fast as before. Surely she was misunderstanding. "But...you have often said you are not a man who wants to be tied down."

He shrugged. "Historically—metaphorically—that's been true, but in the strictest sense of the word, I very much like to be tied—" With one look at what must have been a distressed expression, he apparently decided not to finish the thought. "We can discuss that later. Listen. Veronica...I'm in love with you. I think I have been since that time you slapped me on the Devil's Dirge."

She shook her head in disbelief. Love? Him? Could he truly love anyone but himself?

"I thought I'd already lost any chance at being with you because of all the reasons you have so eloquently stated against me," he continued, with a wry quirk of his brow. "But I wonder if we could move past all that. If we might see where this journey could take us."

Just as she'd begun to recover her breath, it was taken again. "Where...where would you want it to go?" she fretted. "Neither of us really have a home."

"I never have, and I believe your spirit is much like mine. We don't have to settle anywhere, you and I. We can make the entire world our home if we like. Or we can plant our flag if we reach a place that calls to us."

"Sebastian...think about what you're saying. About what this would mean. Can you truly be a faithful man? Because that *is* what I want—what I need. I have a plan already, one that involves my work. I love what I do, and I only want to get better at it. I cannot allow a husband to eclipse that part of myself. The fashion world would certainly bore you."

His arms stole around her, and she stepped into the embrace, daring to hope this wasn't all a fever dream called forth by her inner most yearnings. "I am a sailor, a drifter, and all I need is a North Star, someone to guide me when it is dark." He feathered kisses over her temples, her brow, her hairline, and worked his way down to her lips. "But I am also a man of my word. I will walk in your wake and watch you take flight. I will never raise a hand or even a voice to you. I will cherish and adore you and try to make you fall in love with me every day until you do. I'll let you win arguments at least eighty percent of the time, even though I'm usually right. I will give you two orgasms *at least* to every single one of mine—"

A harried giggle escaped her, and she pressed her fingers to his lips in order to take a silent moment to listen to her heart. "What would I do with such a wicked man as my—?"

Oh God, she'd almost said *husband*. They'd not even discussed what this arrangement would look like on paper.

He held those fingers to his lips, only pulling back to speak. "I would make you a countess again, if you'd allow it. Give you a new name, even if it shouldn't belong to me."

"I would love that more than anything," she sighed, unable to help being swept away by the fervency of her reaction to his words. "With everything that's happened to us both...do you think we could truly ever trust each other?"

"I will strive to earn your trust," he vowed. "But it will take time...time I'm willing to give. As long as you need. Forever, if that is what it takes."

A brilliant smile broke over her features and reached in to set her heart aglow as she saw an identical joy lift his lips. "I think...I would look forward to forever. I'd be much more interesting with you at my side."

"Lovely!" He kissed her, lifting her against his chest. "Let's get married, then! Today, if you like."

She laughed in earnest this time, squirming to be let down. "Do you call that a proposal?"

"I call it a suggestion until I can get a ring." He rubbed his jaw, now rakishly prickled by a night's growth of beard. "Shall we go buy one at the Turkish Bazaar? Or perhaps I should take you to Antwerp or—"

"Take me to bed first?" Sliding her arms around his neck, she stretched up to seal her lips over his in a searing kiss, while rubbing her body against him like a hungry cat. "We could stay there until the train runs out of track...then decide what happens next."

That wicked smile spread over his breathtaking features, the one that'd first arrested her attention so many months ago. "My lady, your wish is my command."

*Also by Kerrigan Byrne*

## A GOODE GIRLS ROMANCE

Seducing a Stranger

Courting Trouble

Dancing With Danger

Tempting Fate

Crying Wolfe

Making Merry

## THE BUSINESS OF BLOOD SERIES

The Business of Blood

A Treacherous Trade

A Vocation of Violence

## VICTORIAN REBELS

The Highwayman

The Hunter

The Highlander

The Duke

The Scot Beds His Wife

The Duke With the Dragon Tattoo

The Earl on the Train

## THE MACLAUCHLAN BERSERKERS

Highland Secret

Highland Shadow

Highland Stranger

To Seduce a Highlander

**THE MACKAY BANSHEES**
Highland Darkness
Highland Devil
Highland Destiny
To Desire a Highlander

**THE DE MORAY DRUIDS**
Highland Warlord
Highland Witch
Highland Warrior
To Wed a Highlander

**CONTEMPORARY SUSPENSE**
A Righteous Kill

**ALSO BY KERRIGAN**
How to Love a Duke in Ten Days
All Scot And Bothered

# About the Author

Kerrigan Byrne is the USA Today Bestselling and award winning author of several novels in both the romance and mystery genre.

She lives on the Olympic Peninsula in Washington with her two Rottweiler mix rescues and one very clingy cat. When she's not writing and researching, you'll find her on the beach, kayaking, or on land eating, drinking, shopping, and attending live comedy, ballet, or too many movies.

Kerrigan loves to hear from her readers! To contact her or learn more about her books, please visit her site or find her on most social media platforms: www.kerriganbyrne.com